To Rita
Dick
Donna
Dale
and Diane

Love to you all

Ted

Y0-ACB-523

RU SP

THE MURDERS ON THE SQUARE

THE MURDERS
ON THE SQUARE

A RED BADGE NOVEL OF SUSPENSE

by Theodore George

DODD, MEAD & COMPANY · NEW YORK

Copyright © 1971 by T. G. Berk
All rights reserved
No part of this book may be reproduced in any form
without permission in writing from the publisher

ISBN 0-396-06406-X
Library of Congress Catalog Card Number: 76-169734
Printed in the United States of America
by Vail-Ballou Press, Inc., Binghamton, N. Y.

THE MURDERS ON THE SQUARE

Chapter One   St. Paul's Square is an island of respectability in lower Manhattan's seething sea of poverty. Not wealth—just respectability. The houses facing the churchyard that occupies a good part of the west side of the Square are havens for pairs of spinsters, schoolteachers, retired Army officers who never rose above the rank of major, and overage clerics who, like firehorses, need the sound of the bells to justify their waning existence. These superfluous souls flock like pigeons to the Square, to live out their lives in search of that crumb of meaning that they had obviously overlooked somewhere along their way.

Only one high-rise apartment house marred the nineteenth-century landscape. Towering over the classic brown stones, it resembled nothing more than a glass filing cabinet with the bottom drawers pulled open. The builder had named it The Hawthorne, but because of the influx of young couples, bachelors, and bachelor girls it brought to the Square and the natural alliteration, the less genteel of the older male residents simply called it The Whorehouse. Those who couldn't bring themselves to think in such coarse terms referred to the glass tower as "that place."

The new apartment house was blamed for all the ills of the world. When Mrs. Hodges in 108 St. Paul's Place, across the square, had trouble with her television reception, it was because "that place" was blocking out the "rays." When Major Lawson's rubber tree inexplicably dried up and dropped its leaves, it was because the new building reflected the sun too strongly into his living-room window. When drunkards slept it off in the churchyard, not an uncommon happening on the Lower East Side, they had been somehow attracted to the area by "that modern monstrosity."

Another thing The Hawthorne brought to St. Paul's Square was murder.

The crime occurred on the twenty-seventh day of October, at eleven-forty P.M. It was a clear, dark autumn night, with an invigorating chilly snap in the air. Although it forbode the winter to come, its very coolness was a pleasant change from the oppressive heat of the Indian summer that had just ended. In the brownstones, many inhabitants had, that night, looked to their fireplaces for the first time since spring. A pleasant smell of wood smoke crinkled in the cold air.

June Corbin was just about as typical as anyone could be of Manhattan's fledgling career girls. A secretary in a branch office of the largest stock-brokerage house in the city, she had lived in New York for three days more than a year. Like many new New Yorkers, she considered herself to be in love with the city. How her parents and friends could bear to remain in Allentown was beyond her.

At eleven twenty-five on October 27, she had been walking up to the street level, from the depths of the Astor Place subway station. She had had a date earlier that evening with one Robert Haraldsen, the son of a friend of a friend of her parents. She had never met the young man before, and went to her appointment with some reluctance. By telephone the night before, he had suggested that they should meet in one of the posher midtown watering places. This event occurred at the appointed time and place; they had two martinis each, and went for a leisurely stroll to the movies. On the way, he "remembered that he had forgotten his eyeglasses," and asked if she'd mind if they stopped off at his place, which, of course, was on their way. Once inside, he poured her another drink and proceeded to demonstrate the talent that had won him a spot on his college's varsity wrestling team. She walked out in a fluster.

It was such a nice night, and her nerves were so jangled, that she decided to walk for a while before boarding the subway train to go home. She window-shopped until eleven, and then, realizing the time, quickened her pace to the subway station, boarded a train, and headed for home.

When she emerged at Astor Place, she felt much better —certainly calmer. She set a leisurely pace walking the four blocks to her apartment on the south side of the square, in The Hawthorne.

As she passed the alleyway between two brownstones five doors down from her building entrance, she heard a slight scuffling. Turning, she peered into the darkness. Spying the garbage cans standing in the alley, awaiting the morning collection, she reasoned that it must be a cat. June lived alone, and had considered acquiring a pet.

"Here, puss, puss, puss. Here, puss," she cooed.
Nothing happened.
Moving into the shadows, she repeated her plea.
"Here, puss, puss, puss. Come to June. Come to June."
She saw only the eyes of her assailant as he leapt up from

his crouch behind the cans. Then he was behind her with his hand over her mouth. He did not lose his grip when she fell forward, but, on the contrary, strengthened the hold by placing his knee in the small of her back. They struggled for a moment. She saw his other hand near her face, and saw a steely gleam as he jerked her chin back and slipped the weapon to her throat. She tried to scream, but the air simply gurgled forth from the rent he had slashed. The idea of dying never crossed her mind. She simply died.

Chapter Two Jane Coleman did not live on St. Paul's Square, but rather a few blocks away on East Tenth Street. Nor could she in any way be related to the Square's aura of solid middle-class respectability. She was, in point of fact, a prostitute. Yet it was in the graveyard on the Square that her life ended.

November 4; eight days after the headlined slaying of June Corbin. It was evening. The temperature had gone down, and there was a hint of snow in the air. Occasional flakes fluttered toward the street, caught briefly in the streetlights, and seemingly disappeared before touching the ground. No longer did people welcome the crisp coolness as a well-deserved relief from the heat. The cold only reminded them that winter was near at hand.

The church clock tolled nine a moment before Miss Coleman locked the door to her four-flight walk-up tenement flat and descended the wide, dirty stairs to the street. She was not an attractive girl, being rather thin and pastyfaced. Her father's name had been Kowalski and her mottled fair skin would have been a familiar sight in Warsaw. Her eyes were too wide-set in her moon face, and her double chin a bit too obvious for her to have ever been considered pretty. A bad case of adolescent acne had left her cheeks pitted—a condition which she remedied with much make-up. Her previously mousy hair had been peroxided to white. In an electric-blue knit dress, chosen to show off what little pulchritude she possessed, and her scarlet woolen coat, worn open, she looked like exactly what she was—a street-corner pickup; a tramp.

Yesterday had been her birthday. She had celebrated in her dingy apartment, her only companion being a bottle of New York State champagne. Her lover, actually what the British call a ponce (he lived off her earnings but only occasionally pimped), hadn't shown up until this morning. When he did get there, he was anything but gentle. Pushing her back onto the bed, he forced himself upon her before she was ready, never speaking, and was getting dressed again before she knew what had happened. Before he left, though, he reached under the mattress to her hiding place and removed the eighty dollars she had earned that week.

She stared at the closed door after he left, still not having spoken. Finally, she went to the bathroom to wash, mentally shrugging off what had just transpired. She was an old pro, having been in the business for four years. The birthday was her twentieth.

Had Jane Coleman been more attractive, she probably could have practiced her trade by telephone, or at least in bars. As it was, however, her market place was the street.

She shivered as she stepped down the concrete outside stairs to the sidewalk. This was no night to go uptown, she thought. Business was always pretty good around Forty-ninth Street—even in a blizzard there was some John looking for a quick one—but not having worked the previous night, she didn't have the cab fare. And nobody was going to get her on a subway, with all those weirdos and juvenile delinquents. So she elected to head crosstown for Greenwich Village. She had invariably been able to hustle up a little action there—mostly tourist or Madison Avenue types on a binge. And it was that much closer to home.

As she rounded the corner of St. Paul's Place, she spotted a lone man strolling slowly toward her. On the possibility that her recent birthday might have brought her the gift of a good trick within walking distance of her apartment, she ambled forward. That this was the same block where a girl had been murdered and mutilated last week, never occurred to her. Business was business. The adding machine in her mind quickly calculated that if this was a live one, she would be able to earn just that much extra tonight.

She drew closer. A fast glance at the man's brown shoes assured her that he wasn't a cop—they always wore black shoes, even when they went plainclothes.

Her eyes sought out his eyes. Seizing them, they held fast. Neither blinked nor looked away until they were face to face.

"Cold out tonight, isn't it?" she began.

"Not too bad, really," he countered.

"Are you just out for a walk?" she asked.

"Unless you've got something better to suggest," he said with a meaningful look.

Returning his lascivious grimace, she nodded in affirmation.

"My apartment is right across the square." He motioned with his head in the general direction of the Square's northwest corner.

Without another word, they started walking. He paused

hesitantly and stopped. "We shouldn't be seen together," he said nervously. "Let me go on ahead and you follow. My landlady . . ."

"Okay," she answered. This wasn't an uncommon request. She waited until he was about ten paces ahead of her and then walked after him. Rounding the corner, she watched as he descended a few steps into what appeared to be a basement entrance. She approached the steps apprehensively—more so when she saw that no light showed. "It's all right," he called upward in a stage whisper. "If we go up from here, we don't have to pass my landlady's place. The old bitch has ears like a cat." She descended.

Coming to the last step down, she paused again, but he held out his hand to guide her through the unlighted maze. She reached forward and put her hand in his. Four steps inside, and she was completely disoriented. She couldn't see a thing. Then, she sensed that he had stopped. Without seeing it get there, she felt his free hand on her breast. "Let's wait till we get upstairs," she suggested in as nice a tone as she could muster, to mask her annoyance. But he only came closer to her, putting his arms around her and pressing her body to his own.

She knew all the signs, all the situations, and how to handle them. Or at least she thought she did. She put her own arms around him and ground her hips. Moving her hands up to his cheeks, she pulled his face to hers and kissed him professionally, using her tongue with liberal, if meaningless, abandon. They clung to each other this way for several seconds, perhaps half a minute. Then, finding his hand, she squeezed it and pulled back.

"No sense getting all worked up down here," she observed. "Let's go up to your place and I'll really show you something."

He pulled her close to him again. Before she could protest, his mouth was on hers. If they already had done their bit, she never would have tolerated this. "My time is worth money," she thought, wondering when he was going to have had enough of this preliminary horseplay and be ready to get down to business. As he kissed her, she allowed his hands to creep up to her neck, where they seemingly cradled her head, keeping it tilted backward slightly, the better to maintain the angle of their embrace. Then she was conscious of his face pulling back. His eyes and teeth reflected what little light there was in that darkness. His hands, however, did not leave her throat. Brutally, his thumbs found her Adam's apple and crushed forward. Her hands and nails sought his face, but before they could reach it, his knee found her stomach. The wind was knocked out of her as she lurched backward. Still his hands did not leave her neck. Bright lights flashed in her head, and she knew she was blacking out. Her breathing had stopped forever before he dragged her to the door. He carefully inspected the street for onlookers before venturing forth, then he carried her across the street into the church graveyard. After dumping her body to the ground among the high stones that he knew would conceal them, he quickly took the pocket knife out of his jacket pocket, cut her throat, and mutilated her body with many quick stabs—the coroner later counted fifty-nine wounds.

Chapter Three   Fewer divorces are granted in the City of New York than in any other major metropolis in the country. Yet, the relatively low price of a plane ticket to El Paso or Reno and cheap lawyers have seen to it that there are more divorced people in Manhattan than there are marriages in most other cities. Janet Carrington had received her Nevada decree four months ago.

It was a traumatic experience for the Carringtons, although it had been building for a long time. It had become a question of which was worse—the cancer or the amputation. To the former Mrs. Carrington, the cure had proved to be fraught with unexpected terrors. Although she and Roger, her former husband, had fought constantly; although they had not agreed on anything that either could pinpoint in more than two years; although their arguments more and more frequently had reached the extreme of physical violence; although there had been no sexual satisfaction for either partner since the earliest days of their ill-fated marriage, still the divorce came as a jolting shock.

To Janet, it meant instant loneliness. However bad the marriage had been, it was nonetheless the status quo. To alter that set of circumstances meant nothing short of complete disorientation.

Make-work became the order of the day. The morning crossword puzzle was a religion rather than a routine. She would no more think of not doing it than she would go out into the street stark naked.

All during the proceedings that preceded the actual divorce, she had enjoyed a feeling of jubilation. As a young girl she had gone to schools in Pennsylvania and had lived with her church-on-Sunday, bridge-on-Wednesday parents in Pittsburgh until her wedding. Then she lived, of course, with her husband. It had not been until the plane ride back from Nevada that her confidence slipped. It was not until then that she realized that she had never before been alone.

There were times when Janet Carrington (she had

elected to keep her married name, her maiden name being Cadanovici) missed the chaos of her married days. The only relief she had been able to find from the spinsterish asceticism into which she had settled had been alcohol. At first, she had taken to imbibing at home alone in the evenings. Then she realized that she was sitting in her sunny apartment on the Square, anxiously awaiting the sun to cross the traditional five o'clock yardarm. Discovering herself in this pretense had led to its abandonment. Now, when the bar on the corner of the Avenue opened at three, she was there. By nine, she was generally so drunk that she was just able to weave her way home.

As she sat in the bar on the afternoon of November 18, she thought about the previous night. The regular bartender had been off (he normally protected her from random pickups, although there had been more than one time when she had wished that he would mind his own business), and she had allowed a rather surly middle-aged man to pay for her drinks and take her home. There, he had made love to her, if it could be called that. They had, indeed, gone through all the physical motions—she had even tried a few things that she had always been too shy or embarrassed to do with her husband. But there had been no real satisfaction. When they finished she had wanted him to stay for a while, but he merely got dressed and left. He hadn't even said good-by. Now, as she thought back on the incident, she could not think of his name. She wondered whether she had ever learned what it was. Rummaging through her memory, she tried to recall any details at all about the three other casual lovers she had had since the divorce, but could remember only one of the men at all clearly—and he was the husband of one of her friends. He had come over to visit her immediately after her return from Reno, ostensibly to "make sure ev-

10

erything was all right." She had offered him a drink, and within two hours, they were both drunk enough to fall into bed together. Immediately afterward, he, racked with a combination of panic and guilt, had apologized profusely and begged her not to say anything to his wife. That was Harry Brown—the first "love" of her new life. That occurrence, like this most recent one, had left her feeling used and hollow.

In any event, Janet knew that such empty encounters were certainly no answer to the disquiet that quaked within her. Although she by no means wanted to remarry just yet, she needed some sort of relationship that at least held the illusion of semipermanence.

She had been staring at her martini as if the answers lay within its oils and vapors, when a vaguely familiar voice said:

"It can't be that bad. You look as if that thing is your last living friend."

She looked up, startled. Standing next to her stool was the man who occupied an apartment two floors above her own. She had seen him several times on the stairs and in the neighborhood stores. They had once been introduced by the landlady, but she could not think of his name. He was, she believed, married.

"Oh, hi there. I didn't see you come in. You're . . . uh . . . Fred? . . ."

"Frank. Frank Harrison. I live on the fourth floor."

"Frank Harrison. Of course! How's . . . it's Milly, isn't it?"

"Yeah, Milly. She's fine, I guess. To tell you the truth, we may live in the same apartment, but we don't really see that much of each other."

"Oh?"

"Yeah. We don't really get along all that well. She's got

her interests, and I've got mine." He raised his glass to indicate that alcohol constituted a good part of his interests.

"Mmmm. I know what you mean. The only thing my husband and I had in common was that he liked to have someone to belt around, and I was convenient. We just got a divorce, you know."

"I wondered why I hadn't seen him around for the past couple of months. That's one thing I can't see—beating up women. The way I figure, if you can't love 'em, you might as well just leave them alone."

Harrison seated himself beside her. For the next two hours (six drinks each) they commiserated with each other. They left the bar together, just before eight o'clock, and walked slowly home. Both were more than a little drunk. When they reached the door of her apartment, Janet invited him inside "just for a quick nightcap before you go upstairs to that shrew." He accepted eagerly. Within fifteen minutes, they were making love on the couch.

This time, she enjoyed it. Here was a man she knew, at least slightly. Here was a man who might just be back tomorrow for more. Here was the possibility of companionship without strings or demands. She did not feel bad when, at a few minutes before ten, he finished dressing and mounted the stairs to his own home. Before leaving, he had asked her to meet him in the bar at six the next night. She had not committed herself further than "If I can make it—" But she knew that the proverbial wild horses wouldn't be able to keep her away. What wild horses can't do, however, a killer can.

After he left, she settled down to her usual late-night routine. Pottering around in the kitchen, she concocted a combination sandwich that would defy imagination—bologna, Münster cheese, peanut butter, lettuce and tomato on pumpernickel toast. After slicing the monstrous-looking meal diagonally across the center, she carried it to the bedroom, snapped on the T.V., and settled in for the night. She was humming happily as she pulled the covers up over her legs and prepared to take the first bite of the sandwich.

Mrs. Carrington awoke with a start when the lock clicked open on the door. The television set was still on, and at first, she thought that the noise she had heard had emanated from it. A quick glance at the bedside clock-radio told her that it was a quarter to one in the morning. Feet moved across the living room, stopping at the bedroom door. A turn of the handle and the door was pushed open. She sighed her relief when she saw a familiar face.

"Oh, it's you. You scared me."

He smiled comfortingly.

"How did you get in?" she demanded as her mind cleared from its sleep.

"I took a key when I left. The one you left under the doormat. Funny how people will lock up their houses like Fort Knox, and then just leave a key lying around outside."

"Well, you had no right doing that! I don't like that kind of surprise. Now give me that key and please leave." She held out her hand to receive the key. He drew closer.

When he reached the bed, however, he did not hand her anything. Instead, he sat down at the edge and tried to embrace her.

"Dear God, enough is enough," she said testily as she tried to squirm away. "Now if you don't give me the key, I'll just change the lock in the morning. In the meantime, I think you'd better get out. I don't want to have to call for help. It could be pretty embarrassing for you."

Resignedly, he reached into his trouser pocket and fished around. She thought he was going to give her the key. She gasped when she saw that what he took out instead was a knife.

"What are you doing?" she demanded in horror. He smiled patiently, then he shot forward, clamping his free hand over her mouth. The force drove her head back onto the pillow, exposing her throat to the ripping blade.

Chapter Four   On the evening of November 18, Police Lieutenant and Mrs. Alfred Zimmerman were dinner guests at the home of Sergeant and Mrs. Robert Donofrio. The fare was lasagna, a dish Mrs. Donofrio took justifiable pride in serving. Born Norma O'Hara, she had never cooked anything more Mediterranean than macaroni before her marriage. In the nine years that followed, however, she had developed such a flair for Italian food that anyone who didn't see her flaming red hair would take an oath that the cook must have been born in Sicily.

The Zimmermans were guests of the Donofrios every other Tuesday night. On alternate Tuesdays, the foursome dined at the Zimmermans' home. Kathy Zimmerman, who had been christened Sullivan, took great pride in her preparation of traditionally Jewish food.

As the wives cleared the dishes from the table, the two policemen leaned back expansively in their chairs and waited for coffee to be served.

"Funny thing, Bob," the lieutenant began, patting his stomach to indicate satisfaction, "You know I only married Kath because I like corned beef and cabbage. So what do I eat every night? Latkes, kishka, blintzes—my own mother wasn't so Jewish. And she came from the old country." This was the more or less traditional joking that followed a meal prepared by either of their Irish wives. Both men were extremely pleased with their spouses, and more than a little proud of how the women tried to make them happy. But to acknowledge this in public, in anything but a joking fashion, would have almost constituted a violation of the unwritten rules of family repartee.

"I know what you mean," Donofrio answered. He put on a thick stage brogue and declared, "Ah, fur a bit o' me mither's own foine cookin'. Me poor mouth wahters at the thought of as much as a biled potater."

The men laughed, knowing that their wives, by this time in the kitchen stacking the dishes in the sink, were smiling as well. They were about to continue their banter, when Robert Donofrio, Jr., the sergeant's seven-year-old son and heir, entered the room. Despite his Italian name, the boy had the red hair and freckles of his mother. Dressed in his pajamas, the child had heard the laughter and was determined not to be left out.

"Yes, Robby?" his father asked. "How come you're not asleep?"

"I heard you laughing. I want to laugh, too. What's funny?" the boy replied.

The two men looked at each other briefly and smiled.

"The only funny thing I see," Zimmerman said, "is a little boy with more freckles than I've ever seen in my life. Where'd you get all those freckles, Robby?"

Blushing, the boy answered, "From Mommy."

"Tell me, Robby," Zimmerman went on, "have you decided what you want to do when you grow up? Last time, you told me you wanted to be a garbage man, and before that, you wanted to be a fireman, and before that you wanted to be a pilot on a spaceship. Have you made up your mind yet?"

The boy hesitated, screwing up his face in overstated thoughtfulness. "I'm going to commit the perfect murder," he announced. "Just like they're always trying to do on television."

He beamed proudly, as the expression on both men's faces revealed that the answer had taken them completely unawares. He suddenly realized that he must have said the wrong thing—neither Daddy nor Uncle Al were smiling any more.

Robert Donofrio, Sr., rose from his chair and playfully swatted his son on the bottom. "Off to bed with you, young man. It's way past your bedtime." His son scooted forth and headed breakneck for his recently vacated bedroom. The father followed to tuck the boy in bed. As he kissed his son good-night, the senior Donofrio said: "And we'll have no more talk about murders, perfect or otherwise."

The perfect murder, Donofrio thought as he lay awake that night, is committed somewhere every day of the week. No, he corrected himself; that's not really true. There just weren't that many murders. You could certainly say that about the perfect crime, though. It was the criminals that were imperfect. If a man pulled a dozen stick-ups, and wasn't captured until the thirteenth, when, as often as not, a liquor-store clerk belted him with a bottle and held him for the police, hadn't he committed twelve perfect crimes? If anybody—a rank amateur even—only pulled one stick-up in his life, and wasn't apprehended right then and there, the odds were very much in favor of his getting away with it. No record of arrests, no M.O. that we could point to and say, "It looks like a job done by Charlie Smith," and the guy could go scot free.

Murder's a bit different, he pondered. Murder is

16

usually a pretty emotional business. A guy kills his wife—the overwhelming majority of murders are spouse against spouse—and before you know it, the poor sap cracks. Forget all this talk about police brutality. Forget the third degree. Forget all that garbage. If the joker doesn't walk right up to the desk sergeant in his neighborhood stationhouse and announce, "I've just killed my wife" (which happens surprisingly often), then all we have to do is subtract one from two and come up with one.

So you put it to the guy. You tell him you know he did it, and in ninety per cent of the cases, he's only too anxious to tell you all about it.

He thought back to a case he had investigated last week. The neighbors reported frequent fights between the couple; the fellow had been arrested twice for beating his wife so severely that the police had to be called in—disturbing the peace—he had lost four jobs in a year. There was one unstable fellow. Donofrio had gone to the man's apartment to arrange for his wife's body to be autopsied. No charge had been made. No arrest had been threatened. A warrant hadn't even been drawn up. But the fellow figured that the cops had come to arrest him, so he just came right out and confessed. Poor bastard. He would probably spend the rest of his life in prison, just because he couldn't stand her nagging any more and didn't have the guts to just get up and leave her. Poor bastard.

But psychos, he thought, they are something else again. They got the biggest headlines. If they didn't have a record, they were the hardest to trace. But at least they usually stuck to one method. Rapists weren't stick-up artists, and stranglers never used a gun. A mugger could no more alter his patterns than a cat could bark.

Sergeant Donofrio rolled over uncomfortably in his

bed, careful not to disturb his sleeping wife. His thoughts had come full circle from his work, to what Robby had said, and back to his work. His latest case involved an obvious psychopath, and he was getting nowhere fast. The first murder had occurred on October 27. The second, on November 4. Both in the same neighborhood. That was the only connection, aside from the fact that both victims were women and they were both strangled and stabbed brutally—mutilated would be a better word. No simple murders, these. They were definitely the work of a madman. A "'normal" person, driven to murder, will stab once, twice, maybe even a few times until he is sure that his victim is dead. But in both of these crimes, the subjects were stabbed over and over again, as if in vengeance. Then, as if that wasn't enough, their sexual organs were slashed apart. Whoever the killer was, he was trying to murder all the women in the world when he picked these two. According to the coroner, the second girl showed signs of having been raped as well, although that was sort of difficult to determine. She was, after all, a known prostitute. Sloppy business, no matter how you looked at it.

He rolled over again, feeling his hip come into contact with his wife's leg. Reaching over, Donofrio smoothed her hair and thought for the thousandth time how like a little girl she looked when she slept. You'd never think she had a son old enough to be getting sassy. As he looked at her, an uncomfortable thought came into the forefront of his mind. He had been thinking it for hours, but had sublimated its recognition. The psycho hadn't done anything in over a week—no, it was fully two weeks since the last murder. If he ran true to form, there would be another victim soon. And neither he nor Al Zimmerman, who was in charge of the case, had a clue. Sergeant Donofrio said a silent prayer—just for some sort of guidance before the killer did it again. He untangled the bedclothes from his legs and rolled over again. After about an hour, he fell into a fitful sleep.

Chapter Five   "Don't take your coat off, Bob," Lieutenant Zimmerman called when Sergeant Donofrio entered headquarters. "We've got another one." Before the sergeant could answer, he found himself being led by the arm back out the door and into a waiting unmarked car. The lieutenant slid behind the wheel, his junior partner taking the passenger seat. As he started the car and eased out into traffic, Zimmerman said, "One-fourteen, this time."

"St. Paul's Place?"

"Where else?"

"Same guy?"

"Looks that way. Victim's a fairly young woman. Divorcée. Fairly recent, according to the landlady. Name's Janet Carrington."

"The landlady?"

"No," replied the lieutenant, glancing over in mild annoyance. "The victim."

"How did we find this one? In the street again?"

"No, that's where this case is different. She was murdered in her bed. No sign of forced entry. I've got the lab boys up there now, making sure. Naturally, none of the neighbors heard a thing. The landlady found her when she brought up her mail. Apparently, her alimony check was sent registered mail on the fifteenth of the month. Landlady knew what the letter was, and knew she was waiting for it. The mailman rang the victim's bell for a couple of minutes, and when there wasn't any answer, he asked the landlady to sign for it. The landlady figured that Mrs. Carrington was probably drunk again—she had been hitting the bottle pretty hard since her divorce—so she brought the check up to her. No answer at the door, so she let herself in. Found the body and called the patrolman on the street from the window. Ozzie Duncan. Remember him?"

Donofrio smiled. Patrolman Third Class Oswald Duncan was a legend on the Force. Not only was the policeman one of the nicest men he had ever met, he was also one of the most luckless. Ozzie Duncan had an incredible knack for just missing. When he took examinations for promotion, he would invariably fail by the narrowest possible margin. When early retirement benefits were announced for the older policemen, it turned out that Duncan had joined the force less than a week too late to be eligible. Even in simple things—if one of the other officers was going out for sandwiches while Duncan was on station-house duty, Duncan would walk in just after the fellow left and miss him. It had become a department joke.

But on the other side of the coin, Duncan was one of the best-liked men they had. People looking for a street number on his beat would, if they asked him, find that he was not content to direct them, he walked them to the door. If anyone were locked out of his apartment, Ozzie Duncan would find him a locksmith, no matter what holiday it might be. People in St. Paul's Place didn't have to telephone the police—they could just stick their heads out of the window and holler, "Ozzie!" and he'd be there.

"Duncan went up, took one look at the body, and called in. Honestly, the way he was carrying on, you'd think it was a member of his family."

Donofrio paused for a moment before he said, "To him, maybe she was."

Ozzie Duncan was waiting for them on the front stoop of 114 St. Paul's Place when they pulled the car into the no parking zone across the street from the building. He walked over to them as they got out.

"Hello, Lieutenant. You're Sergeant Donovio, aren't you?"

"Dono*frio*, Ozzie." The sergeant extended his hand.

"Yeah," Ozzie Duncan replied as he shook his superior's hand, "That's right. Donofrio."

"Ozzie," inserted Zimmerman, anxious to get on with it, "what happened here?"

"Mrs. Carrington," the patrolman began. "Poor woman. How could they do something like that to a nice lady like that?"

"Sure, Ozzie. We feel bad about it, too. Now, what happened?"

At once, the elderly officer became very businesslike and direct.

"Female Caucasian. Age about thirty-five. Divorced about three months ago. No children. You know how it is, Lieutenant. She started drinking pretty much. Oh, not D.T.s kind of drinking. Just more than she ever did before. That used to be her husband's department. He was a terror when he got drunk, he was. Used to beat the living daylights out of her. Well, about six months ago, I don't see him around any more, and when I asked Mrs. Belden, the landlady, she tells me that he up and walked out. Good riddance, too, according to her. Then, maybe three months ago, she tells me that the Carringtons got a divorce. He went to Reno, or some such place, I guess.

"At any rate, to make a long story short, this morning,

21

at . . ."—he paused to consult his note pad—". . . eight fifty-five, I was walking west, on the other side of the park, when I hear Mrs. Belden yelling for me. I cut across the square, and there she is, leaning out of the Carringtons' front window, hollering her head off. I went upstairs to Apartment TwoA, the Carringtons' place, and found Mrs. Belden just about in hysterics. I helped her down to her place on the first floor, got her a drink of water, and told her to calm down. Then I went back up to the Carringtons' and looked around. Nothing unusual in the living room, but when I went into the bedroom, I saw poor Mrs. Carrington laying face up on the bed in the biggest mess of blood that I ever saw. I mean, really, I've seen guys who were pretty cut up and bleeding like stuck pigs, but I never saw *this* much blood. The blood was nearly all dry, so I figured it must have happened a few hours ago, or more.

"I went back downstairs to Mrs. Belden's. She had pretty much calmed down, although she was still jumpy. I asked her to fill me in on whatever she knew, which I told Sergeant Faraday when I called in. I phoned from Mrs. Belden's place."

"Okay, Ozzie," Zimmerman said, not without compassion. "You did a good job. Wait down here for the ambulance. Keep your eyes open. If you see anyone you don't know looking a little too curious, or if you spot Mr. Carrington around, let us know immediately. On second thought, if Mr. Carrington shows up, stop him and bring him to us."

The two senior officers ascended the stairs to the second floor and entered Apartment 2A. Walking through the living room, they entered the bedroom, where they found two laboratory technicians working the room over. They had already covered the body with a sheet.

After greeting the technicians and identifying them- selves, the two policemen went to the side of the bed. Donofrio pulled back the sheet. He quickly turned away. The lieutenant took the sheet from his hand and replaced it over the woman's face.

"Ozzie Duncan wasn't kidding when he said this was some mess," the sergeant said. His partner merely grunted in reply.

"What do you say we leave this place to the ghouls and question the landlady?" Donofrio continued. The techni- cians looked up and frowned at the crude reference to them.

Without answering, Zimmerman led the way out of Apartment 2A, and down the stairs. They paused at the landlady's door. Zimmerman quickly turned to Donofrio. "I've got a funny feeling about this one, Bob. I can't put my finger on it, but there's more here than we're seeing."

"What I saw was more than enough for me," the ser- geant replied.

Chapter Six   The mills of the gods, it is said, grind slowly, but they grind exceeding fine. So too, the Police Department. A case, before it can be presented to the dis- trict attorney's office with a recommendation to prosecute, is made up of an accumulation of perhaps thousands of details. This is the tedium of police work. By comparison, Wyatt Earp had it easy.

And while these details are being sifted, and, hopefully, pieced together into something that makes sense, killers can kill more.

Joanna Coldter, née Simmons, lived, with her husband

Frederick—Rick to her—she hated the name Fred—in The Hawthorne. Apartment 6D was what is jokingly called a two-and-a-half-room studio. It consisted of one large room, a tiny kitchen, and a bath. She had told her friends back in Erie that she had spent half her married life looking for that half room. Perhaps it was supposed to be the closet.

Their furniture consisted of a sofa that converted into a double bed, a coffee table that elevated and folded out to seat six for dinner, three odd upholstered chairs, a television set, and four folding chairs that only left the closet when the young couple entertained their friends. For the privilege of occupying this petite palace, the Coldters paid $168.50 per month, unfurnished. The $85 a week that Joanna earned as a secretary uptown, and the $70 a week her husband grossed as an advertising-agency trainee, barely enabled them to afford even this. "For this my mother sent me to college?" he had complained. "I could earn a hell of a lot more hauling garbage!" But they both knew that some day he would be earning quite a bit more, so they put up with it. They had, after all, only been married for four months.

However miniscule the apartments, The Hawthorne did boast all the modern conveniences that are expected in a new, Manhattan, "luxury" beehive. Central T.V. antenna, self-service elevators (three), laundry room on each floor, a nice view of the Square, a doorman, and an incinerator for garbage, with dump-chutes on every floor.

It was to the incinerator that Joanna Coldter was headed on the night of November 20 when she died.

As was their custom, they had dined late that night. Typically, when they returned to The Hawthorne from their respective offices, they were exhausted. As usual, Joanna got home first, at a little after five thirty. No sooner had she removed her coat, than she went into the cubbyhole kitchen to mix a pitcher of martinis. With both of them working, she honestly did not feel much like cooking on weekdays, and Rick would usually stop on his way home to pick up a pizza, Chinese food, hamburgers, or whatever else he could find to take out. To mix up the batch of alcoholic relaxant that they both frankly needed in order to calm down after a day's work, made her feel that she was not neglecting entirely her housewifely duties. It was a rationalization, perhaps, but neither she nor Rick seemed to notice.

When Rick Coldter slumped home that night, it was nearly seven o'clock. He had worked late again. By that time, Joanna had almost finished her third martini, and after draining the crystal wedding-present jug in pouring him his first libation, she proceeded back to the kitchen to mix another helping. When done, she set the pitcher in front of him on the coffee table, and returned to the kitchen to dish out their dinner—Chinese food, this time —onto plates. She sipped the rest of her drink while doing so.

It was almost eight o'clock when they ate. By that time, Rick was on his third martini, and Joanna, her fifth. Clearing the dishes from the coffee table, she felt hot and slightly woozy.

"Can't we do anything about this damn heat?" she asked as she scraped the plates, emptying the scraps into the brown paper bag in which the dinner had come.

"Not really, honey," her husband answered. "Guess they have to send up a lot of heat so the upper floors get some." He, too, had loosened his tie and removed his jacket. Still, beads of perspiration formed on his forehead. "Why don't you change if you're uncomfortable?"

"I think I will," she said, setting down the dishes, and

leaving the kitchen for the bathroom, where she had hung her nightgown and robe.

Emerging from the bathroom in a flimsy nylon baby-doll that was translucent almost to the point of being transparent, she paused only to allow him to admire her, as she always did, before returning to the kitchen to finish her chores.

"Honey," he called after her, "you just have to be the sexiest thing on the sixth floor."

"Oh," she called back teasingly. "What have they got up on seven that can beat this?" She backed out into the living room, with a toss of her shoulder-length brown hair, and gave her fanny a five-martini wiggle.

"I think I better get ready for bed, too," was his reply.

When he shut the bathroom door behind him, she returned to finish assembling the garbage.

Opening the front door, she called to him, "I'm just going down the hall to dump the garbage."

"All right, but don't be long, sexpot."

She glanced quickly up and down the hall, which seemed surprisingly cool after the stuffiness of their apartment, and seeing no one, traversed the hundred feet to the incinerator, which was housed in what might best be described as a steel-lined broom-closet. The steel on the walls and doors was a concession to the fire laws. Holding the heavy door open with her leg, she opened the chute with her left hand, her right hand forcing the garbage down. She was in this awkward position when she felt the hands reaching around her and cupping her breasts.

"Oh, Rick," she said in mock annoyance, "wait till I get back, at least. I believe you'd do it right here, if you didn't think we'd be seen." The hands left her breasts, but instead of leaving her body, they rose, still under her arms, behind her neck, catching her in a half-nelson. It was not until she felt the thumbs forcing at her throat, hard on her larynx, that she panicked. By then, of course, it was too late.

She was still holding the incinerator chute open when she fainted. Her assailant moved further into the broom closet, closing the door behind him. After forcing her head into the chute so that she was held up by that alone, and his hands were free, he took out his knife, and, stabbing with his arms around her, toward himself, methodically proceeded to mutilate her warm body.

It was like this, hanging like a side of fresh-killed, still gory beef, that her husband found her, not ten minutes later.

Chapter Seven   Lieutenant Alfred Zimmerman finished reading a newspaper article about the incompetence of the police in dealing with mass murderers and threw the paper toward his office wastebasket in disgust. Sergeant Donofrio sat in silence on the other side of the desk. They both watched as the paper glanced off the top of the basket and sprawled itself on the floor. Donofrio rose and put the paper in the can.

"How do you like those guys?" Zimmerman demanded. "Just look at that trash. The idiots tell Carrington we're looking for him. That should make our job easier, shouldn't it?"

Donofrio didn't answer. He knew that none was expected.

"Those goddamn fools," Zimmerman went on. "They've decided that there's one killer doing all this, that he's a rapist, and that the police can't do a damn thing to stop it. I'll bet we get two hundred crank calls today alone. I wish to hell they could have left my name out of it. All the nuts in New York are going to be calling me!"

Donofrio nodded sympathetically. "What do you think, Al? Are we looking for one nut, or for a bunch of people who are using the first murder as an excuse to do away with women they don't like, and blaming it on a nut?"

"I don't know, Bob. It could even be a combination of the two. The M.O.s are similar, but not the same. In some places they're too much alike. In others, they're nothing like each other."

Reaching down into his desk file, the lieutenant withdrew four files. Rising with the files in his hand, he strode to the blackboard that he had set up in his office when he first attained his lieutenancy.

"Let's see what we've got here," he began.

Dividing the blackboard into four vertical columns, Zimmerman headed each with the last name of a victim. Underneath, he first listed the cause of death. All read "Strangulation," except Carrington, in which he wrote "Heart stab." Next, he entered "Where." Corbin and Coleman were both noted as having been found outdoors —"Alley," "Churchyard," respectively. Carrington was allotted "Bed," and Coldter drew "Hallway." The third horizontal slot took the category "Raped." Corbin, Attempted? Coleman, maybe. Carrington, maybe. Coldter, attempted? Wounds was the next category. He quickly entered the data as Sergeant Donofrio read it to him from the coroner's reports. Corbin—sexually mutilated, fifty-eight wounds. Coleman—sexually mutilated, fifty-nine wounds. Carrington—generally mutilated, including sex organs, sixty-eight wounds. Coldter—generally mutilated, twenty-nine wounds, including four sexual.

"Here's something significant, Al," Donofrio said as he

scanned the medical reports. "In the first three cases, the killer apparently inserted his knife in the victims' vaginas, and twisted. He's a real charmer, isn't he? But in the Coldter girl's case, there are a couple of frontal stabs in the region, but definitely no insertion. Likewise," he went on slowly as he checked his premise against each of the four dossiers, "in the first three cases, the girls' nipples have been definitely and deliberately mutilated. With Coldter, one nipple has been pierced, off to the side a bit, and the other wasn't touched. Stab wounds all over her breasts, of course, but not specifically on her nipples."

"You think she might not have been done by the same guy who did the other three, assuming that the other three murders were all committed by the same man," the lieutenant concluded.

"It's beginning to look that way, don't you think? Look at the inconsistencies. Fewer wounds, not of the same type, no evidence of sexual assault that you could hang a case on. Two of the women—Corbin and Coleman—were fully dressed, and Carrington wore heavy flannel pajamas. They all show signs of at least attempted rape. Coleman and Carrington showed definite signs of having had recent intercourse, according to the coroner. Corbin may not have had the rape consummated, but judging from the scratches—made, we are told, before her death—there may well have been an attempt. Yet Coldter, who flounces down the hall wearing next to nothing at all, a sight that might excite a normal man, shows none of the signs of this type of assault.

"In addition, she was stabbed less than half as many times as the others. Look at the numbers: fifty-eight, fifty-nine, sixty-eight . . . The guy who killed the first three women was pretty methodical. Each one was stabbed about sixty times, each one was sexually mutilated—in

29

very much the same way as the others. These would seem to be the work of the same man.

"In the case of the Coldter girl, though, I just can't see the pattern."

Lieutenant Zimmerman gazed at the blackboard thoughtfully. He reached for the eraser on its ledge and removed "Attempted?" from the Coldter rape column and inserted "No" in its place.

"You may be right, Bob," he said reflectively, and started another horizontal column, marked "Date." In it, he wrote the dates of the murders. "This would seem to bear you out, too. Look—eight days between the first two, two weeks between the second and the third, but only two days between Carrington and Coldter. Besides, don't forget, these were the only two that were committed indoors."

"I don't know how valid that last point is," Donofrio interjected. "Remember, as stupid as it sounds, it's getting cold out. If our boy knows his stuff, he's not going to want to do his stabbing through heavy coats. Particularly with the neighborhood as jumpy as it is now. Nobody's going to stop long enough to talk to a stranger. It has to be a sneak attack. And a girl wearing a coat with a heavy collar can hold off a strangler for quite a while."

"Maybe," Zimmerman answered. "One problem with that, though."

"What?"

"What makes you think our man is a stranger?"

"Which one?"

"I don't know. Maybe both—could even be all four."

"By the way," Donofrio added as he rose to attend to his other duties, "did you notice that all the girls have the same initials? Do you think that means anything, or is it just coincidence?"

"Damned if I know." The lieutenant shrugged, making another notation on the board, underlining the initials of each victim. "Damned if I really know anything at this point."

Chapter Eight   In addition to the members of the Coldter and Simmons families who stood at the graveside in Queens, there were five uninvited mourners. Sergeant Robert Donofrio was one of them. Three were reporters, whom Donofrio knew by sight. The fifth was someone Donofrio didn't recognize, but was obviously out of place. A small, scruffy man of late middle age, noticeably in need of a haircut. The first thing that had caught the policeman's eye was the fact that despite the blustery November chill, the man's coat hung open, revealing a tattered gray sweater. A better look revealed that the coat's buttons had come off. Secondly, and much more significant, he did not seem particularly bereaved. Instead, a fire seemed to burn in his eyes, blinding him to lesser emotions.

With caution and tact, Donofrio had approached members of both families and asked them to identify the mourners. When Maude Coldter, the widower's aunt, rattled off the members of her clan in attendance, she had said of the man that he must be a Simmons. But when Grace Simmons, an elderly cousin of the deceased, performed the same service for her own tribe, she attributed him to the Coldters.

It was not until the minister had departed, leaving the families to their private grief, that the man spoke.

"Believe in the Lord, Jesus Christ, and ye shall be

saved!" he intoned, in a much stronger voice than one would expect to come from such a seedy body.

The mourners turned in surprise, each wondering who in the other family, this strange man was.

"Christ, save us now. Satan is afield."

The mourners shuffled nervously. Whoever this Coldter or Simmons was, his actions were certainly in bad taste. Sergeant Donofrio moved quietly toward the intruder.

"The Antichrist has come, and walks the land. God, save your faithful servants. We cannot fight this evil without You."

The mourners, incredulous, began mumbling: "Who is he?" "Where did he come from?" "What does he think he's doing?"

Sergeant Donofrio moved to the stranger's side and took him gently by the arm. "Here, oldtimer, just take it easy. People are staring," he said quietly.

"Let them stare," the man shouted. "All men must know that there is evil in our midst. Only the scourging of Christ can save us. The Antichrist will rule the earth, as he does in Hell. Already it has begun."

Sergeant Donofrio was visibly embarrassed, for now the mourners stared at him as well. Flushing, he reached into his pocket and withdrew his badge. "Police officer," he said with an automatic authority. "Why don't you come along quietly?"

"Come quietly? Come quietly? Sheep to the slaughter come quietly! No! The world must know what is happening! Four girls have already gone quietly. And their souls are in the hands of Satan. I cannot come quietly."

"Okay, fella," Donofrio retorted, his voice stern. "You can walk out of here with me without any trouble, or I can handcuff you and drag you out. Either way. It makes no difference to me." The sergeant opened his coat and jacket, giving the man a good look at the handcuffs hanging from his belt. "The only difference is that if you make me put the cuffs on you, you'll be charged with resisting arrest along with disturbing the peace."

Without another word, the man placed his hands in front of him clasped in an attitude of prayer, and allowed the sergeant to lead him out of the cemetery.

Once outside the heavy iron gates, he turned to Donofrio and implored:

"Look, what good does it do you to pull me in? I don't know what got into me back there. I don't know. Lately, I've been going to funerals and cemeteries a lot. All my friends seem to be dying, anyway. My wife is buried just over there." He waved his hand back toward the fresh grave they had just left. "Just two rows away from where they just buried that poor girl. I was putting flowers on her grave. I do it every month, you know. I joined that party when they showed up to bury her. I was really hoping that one of them could give me a lift back into town. It's almost two miles to the subway from here.

"I don't know what made me sound off like that. Too much death on my mind, I guess. Be a good guy and let me go. I give you my word I won't do anything like this again."

Donofrio considered for a moment. The man had indeed calmed down quite considerably. The fiery gleam had left his eyes, and was replaced by a filmy glass of resignation.

"All right, mister," the sergeant finally answered. "But before I do, let me see some identification. I'm going to take down your name, and if I ever hear of you pulling this kind of stunt again, I'm going to personally ask the judge to throw the book at you."

Anxious to please, the man quickly reached into his hip

pocket and withdrew a dog-eared wallet. From it he took his railway retirement card and a lifetime New York Central pass that bore his picture.

"Peter Volker," Donofrio wrote in his note pad, speaking the words as he copied them. "Retired conductor, New York Central Railroad. Address 216 St. Paul's Place . . ." He stopped writing and stared at the man in surprise. "Mr. Volker, I'll drive you home myself. On the way, we're going to stop off at headquarters. There are some questions we'd like to ask you."

Chapter Nine   "Damn lying cops," Volker spat at Zimmerman. "Your partner here said he'd let me go. Offered me a ride home! Big laugh—a cop doing anything for anybody. Big joke."

They were entering the third hour of Volker's interrogation, and the two policemen were beginning to grow as exasperated as their subject. Donofrio was secretly wondering whether he had, in fact, drawn a blank.

"What were you doing at the cemetery, Mr. Volker?" Zimmerman asked for what seemed the hundredth time.

"I told you. I was putting flowers on my wife's grave. How many times are you going to ask me that question?"

"We checked, Mr. Volker. There weren't any fresh flowers anywhere near Mrs. Coldter's grave, except the ones that were right there."

"Well somebody must have stolen them. What do you expect with the kind of police force we've got around here. Fine thing, stealing flowers off a grave."

"I don't buy that, Mr. Volker," Zimmerman went on. "Where's your wife's grave?"

"I told you that before, too. It's just a couple of rows from where this storm trooper arrested me. To the left as you walk into the cemetery. Mary Volker. Why don't you find the bastard who stole the flowers I put on her grave. There's a criminal!"

"Mr. Volker," interrupted Sergeant Donofrio, "do you have a lawyer?"

"I don't know. Oh, Herman Greenberg down on lower Broadway, I guess. He drew up our wills, Mary's and mine. But that was years ago. Ten years at least. What do I need with a lawyer? I didn't do anything."

"Maybe you did . . . maybe you didn't. Would you like to call Mr. Greenberg? You have a right to, you know. And I'll tell you, I have a feeling you're going to need a lawyer." The sergeant pushed a phone toward Volker.

"Why, so he can charge me more money than I haven't got? I'm not a rich man. I can't afford to go around hiring lawyers. Just my pension from the railroad. That's all I've got. It's hard enough to live on that without making lawyers rich. Why don't you arrest some lawyers? There's a bunch of crooks for you. Three hundred bucks he charged to draw our wills. Highway robbery."

"Would you like us to get you a lawyer from Legal Aid? They're free, you know."

"Oh, yeah. Sure. That's all I need. I've heard about those free lawyers. All they know is 'Plead guilty.' I don't even know what I'm being charged with, but a free lawyer would tell me to plead guilty anyway. No thanks, I don't need any free lawyers.

"By the way, what the hell am I being charged with?"

"So far, Mr. Volker, you haven't been charged with anything," the lieutenant said in a well-modulated voice. "We could hold you for disturbing the peace and you'll spend the next thirty days in jail. All you have to do, though, is answer our questions and you'll be home within an hour."

"But I already answered your questions. I was at the cemetery putting flowers on my wife's grave. As I told the sergeant, I don't really know why I spouted off like I did. Maybe I've seen too many people die. Maybe these murders right in my neighborhood are bothering me, too. I'm not the only one who's upset about them, I can assure you.

"Jesus, it used to be such a nice section, until *they* started moving in on the other side of Second Avenue. People could leave their windows open on a hot night, without worrying that one of *them* was going to break into their houses."

"Who are *they*, Mr. Volker?" Donofrio asked.

The elderly man looked up, as if to say "As if you don't know!"

"You know damn well who I mean. Christ, they can't even speak English. Just yammer, yammer in that Spanish they talk. All they do is come up here and go on relief. And we, damn fools that we are, we let the city give them the money to carry on like that. They don't even try to get work, you know."

Volker leaned forward as if to impart a confidence.

"They take dope, you know. I've seen them. Pick up some of them, and you'll find the guy who murdered those poor girls. They all carry knives. They've got no morals at all. They're just pure evil."

It was not until then that Sergeant Donofrio noticed that the fiery gleam in the man's eyes that he had seen in the cemetery had returned.

"They serve the Devil. Not God, Satan. What do you think they do in those churches of theirs. Not even praying in English, so a civilized man can't find out what

36

they're saying. They're praying to Satan. Servants of evil, that's what they are.

"Now I'll tell you something that you cops were probably too stupid to figure out for yourselves. Or too blind. What did those poor girls have in common, besides their murders?"

He paused for a moment, looking at both policemen to see if they could guess this secret that he had uncovered. When both simply looked at him, waiting for him to answer his own question, he proudly declared:

"I'll tell you what. Look at their names. The girls' names. Look at their initials. All the same. J.C. J.C., can't you see? J.C.—Jesus Christ! Those goddamn devil-worshippers are killing Christ."

With this pronouncement, Volker fell back in his chair, deflated. He continued to mumble what sounded like prayers.

After staring at him for a few moments, Zimmerman motioned his junior partner to step away from the table.

"What do you think, Al?" Donofrio asked.

"Send him downstairs and let's have Collier take a look at him." Dr. Collier was a Police Department consulting psychiatrist. "I still don't know whether he knows anything about the murders, but he sure isn't normal."

Chapter Ten   "I wish you guys wouldn't go around shooting your mouths off to the reporters," Dr. Brian Collier moaned as he sat in Lieutenant Zimmerman's office, waiting for Sergeant Donofrio to arrive. "The next thing you know, the guy is suing the Department for everything up to and including World War Two. Every paper in town has the Volker story."

"Read them again, Brian," Zimmerman answered. "All I can tell them is the truth. We don't know if this is our man, but there are more than a few places where his story just doesn't jibe. *I* never said that we'd caught the killer. If they want to jump to conclusions, we can't stop them. Besides, maybe now the phone will stop ringing with every kook with a parking ticket hollering 'Why don't you catch the Manhattan Monster instead of persecuting us?' Not to mention every spinster in the city calling us to say she just saw the guy peeping in her window."

Sergeant Donofrio entered the room and seated himself by the dusty window. The psychiatrist and the sergeant greeted each other perfunctorily.

"The trouble with that argument," the doctor reasoned, finishing one conversation before beginning another, "is that if we have to let Volker go, they'll scream that we're turning maniacs loose on the streets. And if he is the killer, they're setting the stage for a beautiful insanity defense. It's none of their business if we have a psychiatrist looking at him."

Lieutenant Zimmerman shrugged, indicating that the doctor's last point might well be valid.

"As if that's not bad enough, if he does cop an insanity plea and gets away with it, they'll be screaming for his blood and telling everybody that *we* let him get away with murder."

"What's done is done, Brian," the sergeant interrupted. "Now what do you think? Did Volker have anything to do with these murders?"

"Boy, you guys. You give me a couple of hours with a seriously disturbed man and expect me to put him together like a jigsaw puzzle before you finish your morning coffee. I wish it were that easy.

"What I can tell you is this—he *could* have had something to do with them. Mind you, I'm not saying that he killed anybody. I'm not even saying that he could have killed anybody. We won't know anything about that for weeks, at best. My recommendation is going to be that we place him under observation for thirty days. We should have a clearer picture by then. At least we'll have more time to make a proper examination.

"I'm sorry I can't help you more than that. I wish I could say, 'Here's your man.' But I can't. In the meantime, do us all a favor and stay away from the papers.

"Oh, one more thing," the psychiatrist said as he rose to leave. "If Volker isn't our killer, we're really going to have our hands full."

"How's that?" Zimmerman asked.

"Well, if we do still have a maniac out there, he's going to be pretty sore about somebody else getting the credit. He's going to kill again."

Chapter Eleven Rising from his chair, Zimmerman sighed, walked over to the blackboard, and again underscored each victim's initials.

"You don't really think that has anything to do with it, do you, Al?" asked Donofrio.

"I just don't know any more, Bob. If it doesn't, it is a pretty unusual coincidence. The killer could be some kind of religious nut, as Volker suggested. It could even be Volker. Do you remember reading about that case in Chicago a few years back? The one where the guy left notes: 'Catch me before I kill again'? Maybe Volker wants to tell us that he's the murderer, and he's giving us the reason why."

"That would put us back to a single killer. How do you rationalize the differences between the first three murders and the fourth?"

"It still doesn't have to be one murderer, even if the initials are significant. We could just as easily have one guy who's hung up on J.C.s, who killed the first three girls— or the first two girls, for that matter—and another who saw through this initial business and took advantage of it. If somebody really wanted to get Joanna Coldter out of the way, all he would have to do is add one and one and he'd have to come to the conclusion that there's no time like now. First, she has the right initials. Second, women are being killed like flies right in her neighborhood. Third, the papers have already given a rough idea of the M.O.—first strangling, then stabbing and mutilating. He'd have to conclude that he had a pretty good chance of getting away with it. The papers never printed how many times each victim had been stabbed, which would seem to point to the fact that the first three, with a similar number of wounds, were done by the same person. Coldter, in all likelihood, was killed by someone who had a good reason to want her dead and decided to play the opportunist. Maybe even her husband. He found the body and called us. Maybe he thought he was throwing suspicion away from himself. It's happened before."

"No, I think if he had wanted to kill his wife, he'd have done it in the apartment. We went over that place pretty thoroughly. No bloodstains, no signs of a fight. From what the neighbors tell us, they got along pretty well, what with being newlyweds and all that. I really don't think her husband did it," Donofrio surmised.

"I can't see any doubt that the Coldter murder was committed right there in that incinerator closet. I'm sure that her husband would have found a more convenient place than that!"

"Maybe you're right," Zimmerman conceded. "But don't dismiss the possibility."

"Lieutenant, I don't dismiss any possibilities."

Zimmerman smiled briefly. That was exactly what he would have answered if one of his superiors had given him that warning. He continued:

"Let's go back to the other murders. We'll work backwards and go through everything we know about them. Start with Carrington."

"Okay, Al," Donofrio said as he shuffled through the files. He read in silence for a couple of minutes before he said, "The only thing that seems at all out of place is that she died from the wounds rather than by strangulation. That can be explained, though. The killer probably thought she was dead when he started his whittling. She definitely had been choked. There were bruises all over her neck, concentrated at the Adam's apple—just like Corbin and Coleman."

"There's something else though, Bob. Remember, this was the only one that was actually committed in the victim's home. How did the killer get in? None of the neighbors heard anything. That landlady, Mrs. Belden, seems to know what goes on in that house. You might even say she's a snoop. Yet she didn't see or hear a thing. I'd be willing to bet that whoever killed Mrs. Carrington was someone she knew. She had to let him in the apartment herself. It certainly wasn't broken into. Also, it must have been pretty late at night, and she wouldn't have let in just anybody. So we can rule out the delivery-boy angle. She wouldn't have opened the door for anyone she didn't know very well indeed.

"By the way, any luck on locating *Mr.* Carrington? He's sort of conspicuous by his absence, don't you think?"

"No. Nothing on him yet. He went to Reno, got a divorce." Donofrio consulted the file once more. "He stayed at the Liberty House Motel, just outside of Reno. That's a pretty apt name, don't you think? The divorce was granted on August sixteenth. He stayed there until the nineteenth, then disappeared. He told the manager at the motel that he was going down to Mexico. The manager told the Nevada police that he had been drinking quite a lot, particularly toward the end. He seemed sober enough when he left, but the manager says we can probably find him in some border-town bar, on the Mexican side. Unless he's in jail down there. I already alerted the border patrol and the local police departments in Nogales, Tijuana, Juarez, and all the other tourist-trap towns where a guy who's just shed his wife might go for cheap booze and loose women. So far, no word."

"What kind of work does he do?"

"Not much of anything, apparently. He had inherited some money from a grandfather. He told Mrs. Belden that he was a painter, when they took the apartment." Donofrio grinned as he read the next few lines in the file to himself. "Mrs. Belden," he said, "doesn't seem to have thought very much of his painting. She said, 'It looked like fried eggs with broken yolks and ketchup.' She said she wouldn't have trusted him to paint the walls in her bathroom.

"I gave that information—that he may be a painter—to the Mexican police. He doesn't seem to have to work for a living, though, so I wouldn't count on him trying to sell pictures to eat. I had Donovan and Shea check out the New York art dealers to find out if he had ever sold anything here, or if any of them have a picture of him. The description we got from the neighbors could fit no fewer than twenty million American males. You know the kind —medium height, brown hair, mid-thirties, no distinguishing characteristics or scars. I also cabled Washington to get a good description and a set of prints from Selective Service or the FBI if they have one. He might be just in that age group that managed to sneak through the draft, though—you know, too old for Korea and too young for World War Two."

"That would be just our luck, wouldn't it?" Zimmerman commented.

"And naturally, I have the usual APB out on him around here—New York, New Jersey, Pennsylvania, Connecticut.

"He's not a bad suspect, actually. We know he tended to get violent and take it out on his wife. Officer . . ."— Donofrio searched the file once more—"Vicuto, the night patrolman in the area, had to come up to their place twice. Once, a year ago, his wife called for help. The other time, Mrs. Belden heard the racket and called us."

"Check her bank, and see if they know where the alimony checks came from. That might give us a lead," Zimmerman suggested.

"Didn't have to. Remember, the landlady had one of the checks that had just arrived. I investigated. It comes straight from his lawyer in New York. I also spoke to the lawyer, and he hasn't any idea where his client is. Says Carrington gave him a full year's alimony in advance with instructions to pay her month by month. Carrington told him that 'he might not be near too many mailboxes' for the next year. Seems he was planning quite a trip, even several months ago when he set all this up."

"Speaking of money," Zimmerman interjected, "was

anything missing from her apartment? We could be over-looking the obvious, you know. A really good second-story man with a talent for picking locks could have broken in to rob her, and when she surprised him, killed her."

"He wouldn't have killed her like that, would he? She was cut up like a meatloaf."

"You can't tell. Remember, there had already been two murders of this type. He might have been trying to disguise it the same way we think Coldter's killer had."

"At any rate, we couldn't establish that anything was missing. There was a valuable fur coat—seal—in the closet, a watch by the head of her bed on the night table, a diamond ring on her hand—all there when we found her. There was only about eight dollars and change in her purse, but that's not surprising. She was waiting for her alimony check, remember?"

"Hmmmm." Zimmerman turned to stare at the blackboard. "Well, keep after Carrington. So far, he's the only one who really seems to have any motive. We spoke to some local bartenders who knew her, and they said she had been seen with some men, but not very often and never with the same man twice. We'll keep checking, but that line of investigation really doesn't look too promising."

Chapter Twelve   "All right. Next. Jane Coleman. What have we got?" Zimmerman began again.

Donofrio opened the thickest file. "We've got quite a bit here, but I don't know that it's going to help us that much.

"Jane Coleman," he read. "Born Jane Kowalski, Scranton, Pennsylvania. Occupation: prostitute. She's got a list of convictions that fills most of one page. Ummmm, eleven in all. All the same. Prostitution, loitering, the usual. No narcotics charges—that's surprising. Usually drew suspended sentences or fines. Served ninety days in the Women's House of Detention about a year ago. No arrests since. Either she straightened out, which I tend to doubt, or her stay inside smartened her up on how not to get caught.

"Never married," the sergeant continued. "No children. No next of kin listed. Buried in the public cemetery on Hart's Island. Nobody claimed the body. The tenement she lived in is owned by the Paradise Realty Company, New Rochelle. Some paradise! The place is a pigsty. Bernstein and McMahon searched the place and came up with quite a bit, but nothing seems to spell out anything. No less than seventy-one different sets of fingerprints. Not only did she have a thriving business, she never cleaned house. They're checking the prints but I doubt if they'll come up with anything there. I don't think whoever killed her was a client. At best, we might be able to find out who was pimping for her, and see if he had anything to do with this. Besides,"—Donofrio grinned—"I never object to rousting a pimp.

"There were definite traces of recent, possibly rough, intercourse in her body, but that's no surprise in the business she was in. She might just have had a busy night.

"Nothing from her neighbors. They were used to people coming and going from her place at all hours, although the woman downstairs said she thought she heard a little scuffle the night before. Building has no resident superintendent. There are two other prostitutes living in the building, so I guess the neighbors have learned to look the other way.

"Now we get to the significant part. Her body was found by Patrolman Vicuto at six fifteen A.M., in the church's graveyard. At first he thought some drunk had gone to sleep there. Throat cut, multiple stab wounds, but very little blood. She must have been dead for a few minutes before he cut her up. Larynx crushed. That was our cause of death.

"Here's something interesting. The lab reports that from the way the tips of her shoes were scuffed, she either shuffled badly when she walked, or she was dragged. We checked the other shoes in her apartment, and none showed this scuffing. We can conclude that she was murdered someplace else and dragged into the churchyard. Also, the lack of any blood trail would indicate that the killer used his knife there, rather than wherever he actually strangled her."

"Where do you think that was?" Zimmerman asked.

"Not a clue. I couldn't even guess," came the reply.

"Well, which buildings are closest to where the body was found?"

"Let's see, 108, 110, 112, 114, 116—they're all pretty close. You're right, though. It's a cinch he didn't carry her too far."

"Do we have anybody who's free to check this out?"

"Umm, Howard and Nelson have just about wrapped up a junkie case in the Village. Looks like suicide from an overdose. We'll call it accidental, for his family's sake, but I guess we never will know the truth on that one."

"Right. Tell them to get a few lab boys and comb those five buildings from top to bottom. Tell Howard and Nelson to question everybody. I know most of them have already been asked, but we'll just have to run through it again. Get a dozen John Doe search warrants for anybody who's too uncooperative. Also, tell the lab guys that I want them to keep their eyes open in the basements. It's amazing what people refuse to throw away."

Chapter Thirteen   "Now then, June Corbin. What have we got here?" Zimmerman continued to speak while his assistant skimmed through her file. "Remember," the lieutenant said, "she was the first. The pattern starts here, and there's no chance that the killer was imitating anything he read in the papers—unless, of course, he's been reading about Jack the Ripper. Something drove this nut over the edge. I think we can assume that at least one of our murderers, allowing that there are two, is insane. At any rate, there was something to do with June Corbin that led him to take the plunge. Here, too, much more than with Coleman, we can look for a motive. Despite the way the crime was committed, there's a reasonably good chance that she and the killer knew each other.

"Now what have we got in the file?"

"June Corbin," Donofrio began as if chanting a litany. "Born—Allentown, Pennsylvania, 1949, single, no children. Body claimed by her parents—Mr. and Mrs. Anthony Corbin. Buried in Allentown."

Donofrio interrupted his recital and quickly consulted the other three files. "Lieutenant, you'd better make another line on that blackboard. Maybe this means something, maybe not. But all the victims come from Pennsylvania."

Zimmerman drew a horizontal line near the bottom of the board, and extended the vertical lines to meet it. When his superior had finished this, Donofrio called out: "Corbin—Allentown; Coleman—Scranton; Carrington—Pittsburgh; Coldter—Erie."

Zimmerman entered this information in the appropriate boxes.

"Towns aren't really anywhere near each other," the lieutenant commented as he wrote. "But we'd better check with the local police in each place and see if we can come up with anything the girls had in common. The same school, people they knew in common, if they were ever all on the same bus at the same time—I want to know about it."

Donofrio made a note on the yellow writing-pad on the desk to implement this.

"At any rate," the sergeant continued, returning his attention to the Corbin file, "June Corbin came to New York just over a year ago. Seems to have been a fairly typical career girl. Went to a secretarial school up in the East Sixties. Top quarter of her class. Got a job right after graduation. Didn't seem to like it. She left after a month and got another job—at Scott, Williams and Rutledge, the stockbrokers. We checked with her first employer, a bank. They had her in a typing pool. At Scott, Williams she was a private secretary. Pay was a little better, too. It looks like she just got a better job, is all.

"Neighbors never heard any kind of disturbance from her apartment—the same building that the Coldters lived in, by the way. Her friends—we questioned three of the girls she worked with—said she seemed sort of reserved. She went out on dates, but only on weekends. She never accepted when any of them tried to fix her up during the week. They intimated that she was a little standoffish. No special boy friend that any of them knew about. No pictures of men on her desk. A snapshot of a sailor in her purse turned out to be her brother."

He leafed through the file, and took out the coroner's report.

"According to the autopsy, she was strangled, then stabbed. M.O. would seem to be very much the same as Coleman. Hmmm." He paused. "The coroner says that he found traces of her hymen—seemingly freshly ruptured. The girl might well have been a virgin.

"That would bear out what her parents told us. Not even a steady fellow. No old affairs. No lovers. Nobody with any reason to hurt her. Her parents also indicated that she was a shy girl, bearing out what her friends said. They tried to introduce her to several boys, but she never went along with it."

"Any chance of her being a lesbian?" Zimmerman inquired.

"I don't think so. I asked the coroner and Brian Collier the same question, and they doubted it, too. Besides, she lived alone, and nobody knew of her even having a close girl friend. Even her parents said that she was something of a loner. It's possible, of course. But there doesn't seem to be anything to substantiate it as a probability.

"Well, take her picture around to the queer bars in the area and see if anybody recognizes her," the lieutenant ordered.

"Will do, Al." Donofrio made another note on the pad.

"By the way," Zimmerman said, "have you spoken to any of the girls' priests?"

"Priests?"

"Yeah." Zimmerman smiled at his Italian partner. "Weren't any of the girls Catholic?"

Donofrio smacked his head at his own oversight. "Could be. Coleman used to be Kowalski—probably Polish Catholic. Carrington's maiden name was something Rumanian, I think. Again, she might have been a Catholic. I don't think Coldter was, and I don't know about Corbin. Easy enough to check out, though."

"Bob," Zimmerman began.

"I know, boss."

They both said it at the same time. "Check it out."

Chapter Fourteen "Oh, this is beautiful. This is just great, isn't it?" Sergeant Donofrio moaned to Lieutenant Zimmerman as they sipped their ten A.M. coffee.

"We have a four-state local alarm out for the guy, we have the police in all the airports, railway stations, even the bus terminals looking for him. We even have the Mexican police looking for him. And all he has to do is get on an airplane and go wherever he wants to. That's some efficiency, isn't it?"

"Let's just be thankful he turned himself in," the lieutenant answered. "Remember, he could have been in Brazil by now if he had wanted to be."

"Oh, I know. And however he came to us, I'm glad he's here. But it just irks the hell out of me that with all the APBs we sent out, the guy can just walk right past God knows how many cops as if they weren't there.

"I really can't believe it. He walks in off the street and says, 'I heard about my wife's death. I thought you might want to talk to me.' Honestly, I'm surprised the desk sergeant didn't send him away because his name wasn't on the duty roster."

The superior officer drained the balance of his coffee in a gulp. "You finished?" He nodded toward his subordinate's coffee.

"Yeah," the sergeant answered, wadding the paper cup and tossing it into the waste basket.

"Two points," Donofrio declared as the missile bounced

off the back of the receptacle and fell inside.

Zimmerman reached for his intercom, depressed a button, and spoke. "This is Lieutenant Zimmerman. Would you have Mr. Carrington brought into my office, please."

The two policemen sat in silence while they awaited the arrival of their unexpected visitor. At the last minute, Lieutenant Zimmerman rose and quickly turned the blackboard to the wall. There was a knock at the door before he had finished. Donofrio went to the door and paused, allowing his superior time to get back to his desk. Then the sergeant opened the door and admitted Roger Carrington, accompanied by two uniformed officers. Zimmerman told the escorts to leave.

Rising from his seat, he moved toward Carrington, extending his hand.

"Thank you for coming, Mr. Carrington," he began. "I'm Lieutenant Zimmerman and this is Sergeant Donofrio. We're investigating your wife's case."

"Ex-wife, Lieutenant. We were divorced almost four months ago."

"Yes. So I heard. Please sit down."

Carrington carefully placed himself on the wooden seat facing the desk.

"We'd like to ask you a few questions, if you don't mind, Mr. Carrington. You're entitled to have your attorney present, if you like."

"I don't need a lawyer. I came here of my own free will just as soon as I heard what had happened. Why, am I a suspect? I can prove that I was down in Mexico throughout that part of November, if I have to."

"Mr. Carrington, please try to understand. I'll level with you and tell you Yes, you are a suspect. But so are a lot of other people. I think you can understand that we have to explore every avenue of approach before we can conclude a case like this. To be specific, your ex-wife was brutally murdered, not to mention several other women who were killed in very much the same way. We've had reports that you and Mrs. Carrington had had quarrels on occasion that went beyond the stage of normal husband-and-wife spats."

"You mean," Carrington interrupted, "that I belted her around a couple of times?"

"To put it bluntly, yes."

"Well, that's true enough," Carrington admitted. "Frankly, she was the bitch to end all bitches. Not that I was any angel. But she had a knack of getting under my skin. Believe me, she had it down to a science."

"Okay," Zimmerman agreed, "lots of husbands and wives fight. And it isn't exactly unheard of that they come to blows. But in your case, the police had to be called in on two separate occasions. Once by your ex-wife; the other time by Mrs. Belden, your landlady. That is rather unusual."

"I'll tell you how it was, Lieutenant. To be perfectly honest, I don't hold my liquor all that well. It's funny, though. I could drink all I wanted when I wasn't around Janet, and there was never any trouble. I wasn't exactly teetotal on this trip I took, but I didn't get into a single fight.

"I guess it was just a combination of my boozing and her foul disposition. *In vino veritas,* you know. I wanted to clobber her when I was sober, but I needed that Dutch courage to do it. Take my word for it—if any woman ever deserved to have her head handed to her, it was Janet Cadanovici Carrington."

"Somebody did a lot worse than that, Mr. Carrington." Donofrio commented.

"Yes, so I hear. And, as cruel as it sounds, I can't exactly say I'm sorry. Not that I ever would have done it myself—I don't have that kind of guts, even with a bellyful of booze. I was down in Mexico from the time I got the divorce right up to yesterday. I flew up here last night on Pan Am. Straight from Mexico City. You can verify that with the airline if you'd like."

"We will, Mr. Carrington. Could you give us a detailed accounting of your time for the week of November fifteenth?"

"Easy. I was at Cuernavaca for most of that week. Plenty of people saw me there."

"What was the name of the hotel?"

"There is only one hotel in Cuernavaca, La Paloma. They don't get too many gringos, so they should remember me.

"Later that week—I'm not sure just which day it was—I went on to Acapulco. Stayed in a sort of bar with a tourist court attached." He smiled. "I guess I spent more time in the bar than in the room, anyway. A place called Hotel Benito Juarez. After their liberator, you know. Sort of a Mexican Abe Lincoln. They should remember me—the bartender, Manuel, his name is, had to help me back to my room a couple of times. And just in case he doesn't remember—I'd rather you didn't go this route unless you absolutely have to—you understand—I picked up a girl down there. Barbara Holdakker. H-O-L-D-A-K-K-E-R. I know she'll remember me." He smiled again. "She's from Los Angeles. You won't have any trouble finding her. Just look for a twenty-three-year-old blonde with a thirty-nine-inch bust. You couldn't miss her in a crowd."

Zimmerman smiled indulgently, while Donofrio took notes.

"Mr. Carrington," the lieutenant said, "we'll check out what you've just told us. We won't bother Miss Holdakker unless we have to. Now perhaps you can help us figure out who did kill your ex-wife, if you didn't. To the best of your knowledge, did your wife have any lovers? There were signs on her body of having had recent intercourse."

"The Virgin Queen? Lieutenant, in the last two years of our marriage, we made love a grand total of three times. And that was her doing, not mine. To her, sex was something nice girls didn't even read about, much less do. Oh, it wasn't like that before we were married. No sir. Then, she couldn't get enough of me. But no sooner had we gotten married then she decided that she had outgrown all that. Those are her exact words—'I've outgrown that sort of thing,' " he whined nasally in exaggerated imitation. "She said I was immature in still expecting it. That girl! Do you know, the few times we did do what any normal married couple does, you won't believe what she did afterward. As soon as she was done, she'd race into the bathroom to douche.

"No, gentlemen," he concluded. "If Janet had a lover I'd be very much surprised."

"Well, then. Can you think of anyone else who might want to harm her?"

"By anyone else, I suppose you've still got me down as number-one choice. Let me say this, Lieutenant. I divorced her. I didn't have to kill her. After I walked out and went to Reno, I have absolutely no idea what she did, and frankly, I couldn't care less. Aside from some girlfriends, I don't think in all the years we were married, she ever introduced me to anyone. Outside of family, of course. By the way, I presume they took care of burying her?"

"Yes, Mr. Carrington. Her parents claimed the body. The funeral was in Pennsylvania."

"Yeah, that makes sense." Carrington paused contemplatively. "Honestly, I can't think of anybody who would want to kill her. She was a very cold person, Lieutenant. At first I thought she was just shy. But it was more than that. She didn't make friends the way most people do. Even in college—that's where we met—she hardly knew a soul. No sorority. Nothing like that. She even lived at home with her folks most of the time during those four years. That's what makes me think it must have been a nut who murdered her. She didn't really know anybody."

There was a long silence as Sergeant Donofrio caught up in his note-taking.

"Okay, Mr. Carrington," Zimmerman said as he rose. "Again, let me thank you for coming in voluntarily, like this. Are you going to be in town for a while?"

"I guess so. I'll be going back down to Mexico when I can. But I assumed you'd be wanting me to stick around until you cleared this up, so I planned accordingly. I'll be available whenever you want me."

"Good. Where are you staying?"

"Oh, I don't know. I have to see my family lawyers in a few days to pick up my quarterly check. I have an income from my grandfather's estate, you know. I haven't got a hell of a lot of spending money until then. This flight up here cost more than I thought. All they had on the plane was first class. The most money I ever spent for a steak dinner and two glasses of champagne, by the way. I guess I'll stay at the apartment."

Both policemen were shocked, and showed it. It was Donofrio who spoke first. "Mr. Carrington. Your old apartment hasn't been cleaned up yet . . ."

"Well, I can sleep on the couch. That's where I spent most of my marriage anyway." He paused. "After all, I paid the rent."

"Whew." Sergeant Donofrio exhaled after their visitor

had left the room. "He's a cold one, isn't he?"

"It takes all kinds," the lieutenant answered enigmatically. "What did you make of his story?"

"It seems to add up, if it's true. We'll check out the details, of course. But I have a feeling that they'll stand up. He gave us more than enough bases to touch. Besides, he did come here. All the way from Mexico."

"Your first order of business is going to be to check with the airline. Which did he say it was?"

"Pan American."

"Okay. Also check with them on all their flights leaving Mexico, not just Mexico City, but all of Mexico, for the whole time period from the beginning of the murders to last night. Also find out about the flights into Mexico. Pull any name with his initials—R.C. If he is pulling a fast one, trying to get in and out of the country without anybody knowing it, he might have used a different name, but he probably would have kept the same initials. Also check all the other airlines that fly into or out of Mexico: Braniff, Delta, that Mexican airline—what is it called, Aeronaves?—all of them. When you're done with that, run the same kind of check on flights to and from El Paso, San Diego, any place near the Mexican border."

"That's a big order, Al. It could take time."

"Get a couple of the girls on it. If you need more manpower, let me know and I'll try to get some clerks from the pool."

"What's bothering you on this one, Lieutenant? He doesn't seem any more likely a suspect than a half a dozen other people."

"I know. But maybe he's a little too anxious to cooperate. I just have one of those feelings. He's really going out of his way to appear helpful. Yet all he's done is give us his alibi. And was he ever anxious to give it to us, too. He himself says that he's just about broke. Spent most of his available cash to fly up here. If it had been me, and if I had nothing to hide, I'd just have presented myself to the nearest American embassy or consulate and told them that I was available. The embassy would have contacted us, and we'd have paid his fare back. He's a smart fellow. He would have thought of that."

"I don't know," Donofrio said. "I don't think that would have occurred to me."

"No comment." Zimmerman smiled.

Donofrio grinned in return. "Okay, coach. I've got work to do."

"Oh, and by the way . . ." Zimmerman reminded himself as the sergeant rose to leave, "check out the girl. That Barbara Holdakker. We'll play along with Carrington and not have her questioned, but cable L.A. police to get a make on her. I want to know for a fact that she does live in Los Angeles, that she was down in Mexico when he said she was, and that we can get our hands on her should we have to. Find out everything you can about her, without letting her know that anybody is asking questions. I particularly want to know if she's been in New York lately."

"Are you done?" Donofrio asked sarcastically. "Are you sure you wouldn't like me to fly down to Florida and pull in a couple of astronauts, too?"

"Believe me," the lieutenant said, "if I thought it would bring us one inch closer to solving this case, I'd tell you to do that, too."

Chapter Fifteen "When the hell are we going to get that new computer?" Sergeant Donofrio demanded, more to himself than as a question to which he expected any answer. The sergeant was supervising the roundup of information that the lieutenant had requested, and the complexity was overwhelming. All simple tasks, easily adapted to electronic data-processing, yet by hand they seemed interminable. Seeing the writing on the wall, Donofrio had taken two introductory courses in computer usage over three years ago; the department had announced that it was buying the equipment last year, but it had yet to arrive. With such equipment, he knew, this type of tedium would be reduced to a minimum, while the answers would be available within hours, instead of days. Around the country, other major cities had gone over to data-processing equipment, but New York, with the biggest police department in the country, seemed to be one of the slowest-moving. To date, only the payroll accounts and hot-car lists were computerized.

As the clerks he had "midnight-requisitioned" took the information over the telephone, the mounds of notepaper grew to staggering proportions. "This place looks like a betting parlor," the sergeant mumbled under his breath. Impulsively, he picked up the telephone and dialed 2471, his boss's extension.

"Hello, Al?" he asked when the lieutenant answered.

"Yeah, Bob. What's the matter?"

"Have we got enough in the budget to get this job done in a hurry?"

"What do you have in mind? More warm bodies?"

"No, I want to take this paperwork over to one of those computer service places uptown, and let them run it. We'll have our information within twenty-four hours. The way we're going, it might take the rest of the week."

"Back on that kick?" The lieutenant and the sergeant had discussed data-processing equipment before. Although agreeing in principle that it would make their jobs easier, the lieutenant didn't share his partner's belief that the work couldn't be done without it. "I don't think so, Bob. I'm sorry."

"Oh, come on, Al. Why not?"

"It's not the budget. That information is confidential. We can't trust a third party to keep it that way."

"Oh, Al! These outfits are thoroughly respectable. I'm not going to shop around for the cheapest, you know."

"We can't take that chance, Bob. I'm sorry."

After working with Al Zimmerman for six years, three of them as his sergeant-partner, Donofrio knew when he could argue no further. The tone in Zimmerman's voice indicated that that point had just been reached.

"Okay, Al. I should be coming up for air around Sunday." The sergeant hung up. He stared at the phone for a moment, then turned back to the horde of clerks in the large room he had been assigned for this task.

"How are we doing, troops?" he asked the room.

The glares from the exasperated upturned eyes were the only response.

"I know how you feel. Just keep at it."

In bed that night, Sergeant Donofrio dreamed that he was being drowned in an ocean of paper.

Chapter Sixteen   There was a time when, it is said, if you could use your fists, sign your name, and direct traffic, you could qualify for the New York City Police Department. They also say that it didn't hurt if you were Irish. Those days, fortunately, are gone forever.

Today, many of the new recruits of the Police Department have had some college. And even those who haven't, soon find that if they really want to progress in their chosen career, they had better start taking night courses.

Detective Third Class Miguel Rodriguez was one of this new class of policemen. Born in Puerto Rico, he had arrived in New York during a January blizzard twelve years ago. He was seventeen years old and had come to the land of opportunity. The taxi ride from the airport to his cousin's crowded apartment in Spanish Harlem had cost him fifteen dollars. That was what the driver had told him it cost, and he hadn't known enough to argue.

The following morning, he took his remaining four dollars and bought a snow shovel. By the time he had been in New York City for twenty-four hours, he had earned thirty-one dollars.

On his second day in New York, he found a job in a local grocery store. Thirty-five dollars a week, Monday through Saturday, and he could take home the overripe fruit and vegetables.

On his third day in the city, Miguel Rodriguez visited the admissions office at the City College of New York. He had written to them from San Juan and arranged to establish residence so he could enroll. It was a disappointing day, for he had neglected to tell them that he could not speak English. The letter, along with a warm recommendation, had been written by his high school teacher. Impressed with the boy's sincerity, the admissions officer arranged for him to take English for Foreigners at night, five nights a week, starting in ten days.

By the time the summer session started that June, Miguel Rodriguez was ready.

It had taken him six years of night school to finish his college education. Six years of working in the grocery store during the day and going to school at night. But those years had taught him that the way he could better his people's lot would be to join the police force. He signed the application forms the day after he was graduated.

Rogriguez' decision to become a police officer had not been a popular one with his friends and family in Spanish Harlem. The police, to them, were a major part of their view of the outside world—the world that held them down in bondage. Police were people who broke up their parties, arrested their sons and daughters, and generally told them what they could not do. They were the whip of the oppressor. The young man, however, had a slightly different view. Although he sympathized with his compatriots, he had seen too many instances where a policeman pulled in someone simply because they couldn't understand each other.

But this was minor. The thing that had really made up Miguel's mind to join the force had been much more grave. There was, living on 113th Street, a young man who everybody called "Luis el Loco."

Luis, as his nickname would indicate, was not quite normal. He earned what living he made by carrying crates for the markets that nestled under the New York Central tracks over Park Avenue. Most of the time, Luis presented no problem. But every now and then, some bored workmen would slip some rum into his Coca Cola, and Luis would perform like a circus bear.

On the day in question, Luis had become drunk from the spiked Coke. But this time, even his limited intelligence had enabled him to see through the laughter to the jeers. When he realized what was happening to him, he didn't like it. With a single sweep of his huge paw, he fractured the jaw of one of his tormentors in three places. The others cursed him, and a loud ruckus ensued. Unfortunately for the youth, a rookie patrolman turned the corner just at that point. The patrolman spoke absolutely no Spanish. Luis panicked and ran. The patrolman gave chase.

The bystanders who thronged the crowded marketplace saw what was happening, and when the officer drew his gun and ordered Luis to halt they tried to stop it. "Don't shoot him," they implored. "He's crazy. He doesn't know what he's doing. He doesn't understand." But all the pursuing policeman could comprehend was that a lot of people were shouting in a language he couldn't understand. He thought they were shouting at the man he was chasing, as people shout after a fleeing thief. When the chase ended, the rookie stood over the fallen body of Luis el Loco, writhing in agony on the sidewalk. Luis was not killed, but he would never use his legs again.

Miguel Rodriguez joined the Police Department to help prevent this kind of tragedy.

But just as the Army seems invariably to place drafted lawyers in the Medical Corps, and lab technicians in the Infantry, so too the Police Department had never stationed Rodriguez in a Spanish-speaking area. He still believed that some day they would. In the meantime he learned. In Greenwich Village, his first assignment, he had learned how to be a patrolman. Now, in Homicide South, he was learning how to be a detective.

It was in this capacity that he was stationed in St. Paul's Square, as part of what had become the almost permanent stake-out that had been set up in the area to prevent further crimes. The stake-out would remain until the killer had been apprehended.

It was in this watchdog role that Rodriguez was serving when he was told to keep a particular eye on Roger Carrington. When the facts of Carrington's renewed occupancy of the old apartment were conveyed to the young detective, he was even more appalled than Sergeant Donofrio had been.

"*Dios Mio,* the man is a ghoul," had been his first reaction.

"He certainly isn't normal, Mike," came the reply from Lieutenant Zimmerman, who had assigned him the task. "That's why we want to keep him under surveillance."

But the first night, Rodriguez had nothing to watch.

"Nobody went near that apartment last night," he reported when he called in the following morning, before going off duty.

"Maybe Carrington changed his mind. Maybe he finally started to feel something for what had happened there."

"That wouldn't surprise me. Maybe he's not as cold-hearted as he'd like everyone to think he is."

"Did anything else unusual happen on the Square last night?"

"Yeah, I saw a bunch of cops on stake-out. By the way, where do you think Carrington went?"

"Don't know. We should have had him tailed when he left here, I guess."

Rodriguez made a mental note not to make this error when he held a position of authority.

"What do you want me to do now?" the young detective inquired.

"Same thing. You relieve Taylor tonight for stake-out duty. Same time as last night. If Carrington does show up, though, call in immediately."

"Okay, Lieutenant, will do."

The following night, when Carrington still hadn't showed up where he had said he'd be staying, Zimmerman and Donofrio began to get a little worried.

"Bob, how are you coming with the paperwork?" the lieutenant asked.

"Well, it's all been collected. We're in the process of sorting it out."

"How long do you think it's going to take?"

"A couple of days more. Why?"

"Because I've got some more for you."

The sergeant groaned. "What now?"

"Well, we'll try the easy way first. I want every hotel in the city contacted to see if Carrington has checked into any of them. He never did show up at the apartment. That was Rodriguez on the phone. Not a sign of him. Hopefully, he registered under his real name. Otherwise, we're going to have to run the initials route again."

The sergeant groaned again. "New York has a couple of thousand hotels. There must be an easier way to earn a living," he complained.

"I certainly hope so, for the rest of the world's sake," Zimmerman answered. "Again, I don't want him rousted. I'd just as soon he didn't even know that we want to keep an eye on him. Although if he's smart, he'll have already realized that. Maybe that's why he's given us the slip."

"Why don't we just put out an APB on the guy? That would be the easy way, and every cop in town would be looking for him."

"Too easy for one of them to go wrong. He slipped through the APB at the airport, remember? Besides, I don't want any eager-beaver rookie pulling him in. Also, I don't just want to know where he is now, I want to know where he's been for the past couple of days. It's much easier to get that kind of information by subtlety. Once we know where he is, we can ask him to stop by on some pretext or other, and find out that, too.

"Any questions?"

"Yeah. When are we going to get that new computer?"

Chapter Seventeen "Don't tell me," Lieutenant Zimmerman said as Dr. Collier entered his office the following morning. "Volker confessed and we can all go home and get some sleep."

"Not a chance, Al," the doctor answered, smiling wryly as he seated himself.

Something, Zimmerman knew, was up. The psychiatrist had made a special trip to see him, and, without prior warning or trying to set up a meeting, announced his presence to the desk sergeant. He had then requested an immediate audience with Zimmerman.

"Well, you are here to talk about Volker, aren't you?"

"Yup." The doctor wriggled in the wooden seat to get comfortable. "I'm afraid I've got some bad news for you. Volker didn't do it."

"That's a pretty strong statement, Doc. You mean, you don't think he did it, don't you?"

"Nope, I mean he didn't do it. Couldn't have."

"Look, just because he may have some kind of cockamamy alibi, that doesn't mean that we can't break it.

We hear more wild stories around here than they show on television, you know."

"I wish that were all it was. No. Volker, as I said, could not possibly have killed anyone by strangulation."

"Well, why the hell not?"

"Simple. As you probably already know, when we take someone in for psychiatric examination," the doctor explained as he lit his pipe, "we first run a complete physical examination. It's often very useful in understanding what's going on inside the patient's head, to know first what's happening in the rest of his body. I'd like a dollar for everybody whom I've examined with 'imaginary pains' that their regular doctors couldn't diagnose, where we found an overlooked organic cause. I'll tell you, general practitioners these days aren't what they used to be. All they want to do is farm out their responsibility. I remember one case, honest to God, where the patient had a hairline fracture of his knees. Both of them. His family doctor, some old coot out in Brooklyn, took a set of X-rays that looked like he did them with a Brownie. He couldn't find anything, so he jumped to the conclusion that his patient couldn't walk because he had bats in his belfry. It's a good thing we took our own X-rays. Two beautiful fractures—a matched pair. No wonder the guy couldn't walk."

He paused and relit his pipe. Lieutenant Zimmerman seized the opportunity to cut off the doctor's monologue. "What does this have to do with Volker, though? I can't see the connection."

The doctor exhaled a cloud of blue-gray smoke. "Simple," he replied. "We've been looking for a psychological framework in Volker's case. A framework that would include a possibility that he was a murderer. And we indeed found a very unstable man. With another few weeks of examination, I think we probably could have established that he had an emotional make-up that would not preclude his committing murder. As I said, however, we did a physical examination on him and looked up his past history. In 1941, the patient was a checker in the freight yard. It seems he had an accident at that time. A crate fell on his left hand, breaking three fingers and the thumb. The crate also severed three tendons. The bones were set and healed, but tendons, when cut, never wholly regenerate. That's why they gave him a less strenuous job. First, he sold tickets in Grand Central Station. Then, they put him on the New-York-to-Buffalo run as a conductor. That's where he worked from 1948 to his retirement two years ago. During that time, he regained the use of those fingers, but never the strength they once had. In short, Lieutenant, Volker doesn't have the strength in his left hand to strangle a canary, much less a grown woman. He's not your man."

"You're absolutely positive about this?" the lieutenant asked, hoping against hope that the psychiatrist had something else up his sleeve.

"Absolutely."

Zimmerman leaned forward at his desk, resting his forehead on his hands in defeat. "What are you going to do with Volker?" he finally asked.

"Release him, of course. We were only examining him because he was a suspect in your case. Now that any chance of him being guilty can be ruled out, what reason could we have for keeping him locked up?"

"You said he was a sick man. Don't you want to keep him under observation for the full thirty days, at least?"

"Al, you know we can't do that. We can't just snatch people off the streets because we think they're disturbed. If we did, we'd have more people in institutions than you have outside. Anyway, why should you want us to keep Volker? You know he's not the man you're looking for."

"A couple of reasons, Doc," Zimmerman answered, trying to keep a pleading note from creeping into his voice. "First, as you yourself pointed out the last time you were here, if we turn him loose, the newspapers will have a field day. Second, although we never let up in our investigation, we haven't found anybody else we can suspect. Not really. Certainly not to the point where we could make an arrest—even a loitering or vagrancy pickup for the purposes of questioning. We have been trying too. We just keep coming up empty. This means two things. That the papers will hit us twice as hard, and that the real killer, or killers, as the case may be, will be tipped off that the heat is back on him. As long as he thought we had somebody we were trying to crack, he felt safe. Now, we're telling him to be on his guard again. That makes our job that much harder. Third, while we had a suspect in custody, the cranks eased up on the telephone. If it gets around that we let Volker go, every nut in the city is going to get back on the phone to report shadows in the back yard and cats on the fire escape. That switchboard out there just isn't going to stop!"

The lieutenant paused to allow the psychiatrist to weigh these arguments.

"Al, I appreciate the position you're in. Believe me, I sympathize. But I'm afraid that I can't go along with you. Remember, I told you you shouldn't have talked to the newspapers in the first place. Also, there's a matter of medical ethics here. We can't just use beds that are reserved for mental patients—the few beds that we have—to sequester guys like Volker when a lot of other people need them more. I know that this isn't making your job any easier. But no matter how I look at it, that's not my job." The doctor grinned. "Unless, of course, you'd like to take a little rest cure yourself."

"I'm beginning to think I may have to take you up on that before this case is over, Brian." Zimmerman's lips twitched in resignation. "Well, better luck next time."

Chapter Eighteen   From the *New York Daily Tabloid:*

COPS CLEAR KILLER SUSPECT

December 8. Peter Volker, a sixty-three-year-old retired railway conductor, was released today from Bellevue Hospital's psychiatric ward. Volker, who lives at 216 St. Paul's Place, about a block from the Manhattan Monster's stomping grounds, had been held for observation in Bellevue by the police since he was picked up on a disorderly conduct charge on November 24.

At that time, the police indicated that they suspected Volker in connection with the St. Paul's Square murders of last month. When asked for comment on this most recent development, Lieutenant Alfred Zimmerman of Manhattan Homicide South, who is in charge of the investigation, said: "We are thoroughly convinced that Peter Volker had absolutely nothing to do with last month's murders. Several unusual coincidences that led us to suspect Volker in the first place, turned out to be nothing more than that—coincidences."

Zimmerman declined to describe these "coincidences" or answer any further questions. Just what it was that caused the police to suspect Volker in the first place, and what changed their minds, will remain a mystery.

In an exclusive interview he granted us, however, Volker, a widower with no children, told this story:

"All I did was go to my wife's grave to bring flowers. The Coldter girl's funeral was going on at the same time, and when I went over to ask someone there for a lift back to the city, that cop arrested me.

"They tried to get me to confess. They tried everything they could to make me tell them I killed those girls. They did things you wouldn't believe. But I couldn't tell them anything, because I didn't do it.

"They had to arrest somebody, I guess, so they decided to pick on me," Volker concluded. "What can an old man do to protect himself against these brutal cops?"

The police declined to comment on Volker's charges of brutality, and also refused to disclose whether there were any further developments in the case.

Following this, the *Tabloid* ran a history of the St. Paul's Square murders, with the now-standard box-score of the victims. At the lower left-hand corner of the page, in italics, was a small notice: "Peter Volker's whole story, in his own words, will appear in Sunday's *Tabloid*. Don't miss it."

From the editorial page of the *New York Daily Tabloid*, December 8:

PROTECTION FROM WHAT?

The charter of the Police Department of the City of New York, would have us believe that the purpose of the police is the "protection of the citizenry." In this ancient document, which predates the American Revolution, the obligation and duty of the police to protect us from the lawless and the violent, is clearly spelled out.

In the light of recent developments, particularly in the case of Peter Volker, we can only raise the question: "Who is going to protect us from the police?"

While an insane killer still walks the streets, no doubt in search of his next victim at this very moment, the police prefer to persecute the old, the lame, and the innocent.

It is almost a month since the Manhattan Monster first struck. In this time, he has felled three more young women, all within a one-block radius of the first murder.

The police, the so-called "New York's Finest," would seem to be powerless to protect the citizenry from this kind of onslaught. They prefer to "protect" us from harmless old men.

And why not? It must be a lot easier than catching killers.

"Jesus," Donofrio exclaimed. "They didn't pull any punches, did they?"

"Well, we expected it," Zimmerman said.

"I just can't understand those newspaper guys," Donofrio continued. "You know Handeller and Nally—the guys from the *Tabloid* who hang around the squadroom. They know what it's all about. How the hell can they write garbage like this?"

"It's their job, Bob. Besides, it's not Handeller and Nally who write this stuff; it's some guy sitting on his can back at their office. All Handeller and Nally do is phone the stories in."

"You're defending them, Al? How can you? You know how wrong they are. How do they expect people to cooperate with the police, when they write trash like this?"

"Trash or no, they're right about one thing."

"What's that?"

"It's been about a month now, and we haven't caught any killer in this case."

Chapter Nineteen   Zimmerman and Donofrio were not the only ones who had winced at the jab of the *Daily Tabloid*. Miguel Rodriguez, too, had mumbled a few well-chosen imprecations at the newspaper's editors. Although most members of the police force had been able to shrug off the editorial tirade, as they had done many times in the past, those men attached to Manhattan South Homicide still smarted.

For Rodriguez, it had been worse. In most neighborhoods, people were generally content, despite the rages of the press, to write off the police as a group of typical civil-service incompetents who, however muddlingly, nevertheless did manage to do their jobs. In Spanish Harlem, where Rodriguez continued to live, despite his elevation in social status and salary, the police were still enemies. And if there was an opportunity to demonstrate to him that he had indeed chosen the wrong career, it was not to be overlooked. His neighbors had not been at all gentle in their chiding, either. No fewer than a dozen of them had seized the chance to read the *Tabloid* editorial to him, despite his protests that he had already read it. His neighbors, of course, had no way of knowing that he was him-

72

self assigned to the case. And the fact that he had been frankly ashamed to reveal this to them made him feel even worse.

The teasing he had taken gnawed at his growling stomach as he rode the subway down to Astor Place that evening. He had been too upset to eat his late-afternoon breakfast, and his innards had begun to rumble in protest. He thought of grabbing a quick frankfurter at the stand near the subway station, but decided against it. That would only make him feel worse. Instead, he bought a packet of six peanut-butter-and-cracker sandwiches, which he planned on munching as he walked his stake-out beat.

The stake-out had been set up to cover the most ground with the fewest men. This was fairly typical in as undermanned an operation as most police departments were. In addition to the patrolman who normally walked the larger beat, two detectives were assigned to the area. These men walked, in shifts, around the clock, circling the tiny park that was St. Paul's Square. One pacing clockwise, the other counterclockwise, they passed each other twice during each circuit. In addition, an unmarked radio car with two other detectives had been detailed to cruise a five-block area surrounding the Square, on its fringes. The radio car toured the Square itself about every forty-five minutes.

Under good conditions, the job of being on stake-out is unenviable. When the weather is inclement, it can be downright pitiable. This had all the earmarks of being a bad night.

All that afternoon, the sky above Manhattan had been graying. Curiously still, the air had a distinct odor of the accumulated stink of the city's airborne effluent. Yet it was not the smoke and smog that gave the sky its foreboding quality. It was just cold enough, and just warm enough, for snow.

Miguel had seen this when he boarded his subway train at 125th Street. When he emerged at Astor Place, he saw that the sky had lightened noticeably, but without relieving the anticipation of the weather to come. It reminded Rodriguez of a man taking a deep breath prior to sneezing. As he relieved Arnie Taylor, the day man on the stake-out, they exchanged the customary pleasantries and inquiries into what had happened. As usual, nothing had.

Rodriguez watched the other detective disappear around the corner on his way back to the station house to make his report before going home for the night. When he could no longer see Taylor, Rodriguez noticed that the first few flakes of winter were already descending.

Sighing to himself, he lifted the collar of his coat to shield his exposed neck, and began to walk his rounds.

He walked slowly, as he had been taught, scanning the buildings and the park with what must have been a 160-degree sweep of his eyes, walking on the park side of the street for a better view of the houses. After the first few days on a stake-out, any stake-out, it was as if you had never stopped. These footsteps that he made now were nothing more than a continuation of those made the previous night. Sentry duty in the army was probably worse, he comforted himself. But only because you had eleven pounds of rifle on your shoulder. Otherwise it was the same.

As he turned the corner, he saw Gus Thomas (it used to be Tomaschek, Gus had told him) approaching. Gus was the other half of the night shift covering the park. They both raised their hands in recognition at about the same time. At least I'm not alone out here, Rodriguez thought.

"*Que pasa*, Mike?" Thomas greeted.

"*Que pasa* yourself," Rodriguez answered in mock brusqueness. "This is no night for a Latin boy like me to be out on the streets." He pulled his collar up further and looked up at the streetlight, in whose beams the falling snow was clearly visible.

The other policeman looked up as well. "Nor for me, *amigo*. I don't like it any better than you do." He paused to study the falling flakes. "It looks like it's getting harder, too."

"Yeah, Gus. That's all I need. You know, in San Juan, it's always eighty degrees and sunny. Every day. Eighty and sunny. You never saw a more beautiful climate in your life."

"Then why'd you leave?"

"Man, you can't have good weather *all* the time! It gets boring."

Both men laughed and continued on their ways. Rodriguez told himself that he should have known to wear a scarf, and pulled his coat collar up once more in an attempt to achieve maximum protection from the cold. It did very little good. No matter how long he stayed in New York—if he spent the rest of his life here—he knew that his blood would still cry out for the warmth of the tropics.

He turned the corner and prepared for the long walk east to west. The north-south blocks were much shorter, and better lit. His eyes quickly grew accustomed to the darker side-street, but he still had to blink and try to sharpen his focus when he heard a noise in the alley between 140 and 142 St. Paul's Square South. He crossed the street toward the sound, quickly yet quietly, walking on the balls of his feet. He peered around the corner, past the garbage cans, into the darkness. At first he saw nothing at all. Then, just as he was about to turn away and write off the noise to a foraging alley cat, he saw the figure rising. It was so dark he could not see if it was a man or a woman, or if the figure was facing him or turned the other way.

"I'm a police officer," he called into the darkness, his own voice sounding terribly loud in the silence. "Please come out here."

The figure moved sharply and Rodriguez quickly withdrew his snub-nosed pistol from its shoulder holster. The figure stooped as if to pick something off the ground. Rodriguez saw a metallic glint.

"*Policia. Cuidado. Ven aquí,*" Rodriguez ordered.

"Damn spic, coming around here and telling white people what to do," a man's voice replied.

"I'm a police officer, and I have you covered. Come on out here with your hands on top of your head. Now!"

The sound of the shotgun exploding in the narrow confines of the alley broke a window in 142 St. Paul's Square South. Rodriguez never heard it. The fast-flying pellets had effectively decapitated him before the sound reached his body.

Chapter Twenty   Detective Third Class Gustav Thomas had no sooner heard the explosion than he was running at top speed toward it. As he rounded the corner, he could see a running figure at the opposite end of the block, heading east, away from him. He put on a burst of speed of which he frankly would not have believed he was capable, and narrowed the distance quickly. The fleeing form, now clearly visible as a man, reached the corner of First Avenue and paused. Traffic was heavy and he hesitated before rushing forth into its flow. Thomas, however, kept coming at full throttle. The detective was less than two hundred yards away when he shouted:

"Police officer! Halt! Stop or I'll shoot!"

He had withdrawn his revolver while running.

The man wheeled on his heels and let loose another burst with the shotgun.

Thomas, as soon as he saw the weapon, threw himself flat on the sidewalk. One of the pellets grazed his left shoulder, running a furrow down the arm to the elbow, but otherwise he was unhurt. The policeman immediately got to his feet again and resumed the chase. He could not fire, for fear of hitting one of the passing automobiles in the background. He held close to the line of trees on the sidewalk so that if the shotgun wheeled around again, he would have some protection.

An opening appeared in the flow of cars and the pursued man darted across the street, continuing east. By the time Thomas reached the corner, he could no longer see him.

Without wasting more than thirty seconds in this search, Thomas turned and trotted back up the block about a third of the way, to something that had caught his eye. Rodriguez's body was barely recognizable. It was only the .38-caliber Police Special revolver in the corpse's right hand that told Thomas that this was the other half of his team.

Thomas did not pause to check Rodriguez's pulse, to make sure he was dead. He could not possibly have been otherwise.

Instead, he raced to the police call-box at the corner. It was only when the desk sergeant at the other end of the line answered that Thomas realized that he was panting so hard that he could hardly speak.

"This is Detective Third Gus Thomas on stake-out in St. Paul's Square," he gasped into the phone. "Somebody just blew Rodriguez's head off with a shotgun. I'm at the corner of First Avenue and the Square. The southwest corner. Car three-thirty-one is in the area somewhere. Get them over here. I think we may still be able to get the guy. Tell Zimmerman," he demanded, almost as an afterthought. Only then did he go back to look after his fallen friend.

Chapter Twenty-one The patrol car pulled up to the curb where Detective Thomas stood waiting, less than two minutes after he hung up. Although Thomas's initial intention had been to return to his partner's body, he simply had not been able to bring himself to return to the gory scene. Instead, he waited by the call box for assistance.

"What's going on, Gus?" Detective First Class Arthur Styler asked as he got out of the car. His own partner, Detective Third Class Stanley Kellogg, remained seated behind the wheel, the car's motor still running.

"They got Rodriguez," Thomas replied. "Shotgun. The bastards blew his head off." The enemy was always "they." It was not one man who had killed the policeman, it was the vast unseen army with which his job required him daily to do battle. "One guy. I chased him, but he got away through the First Avenue traffic. He crossed the street and lost himself in one of those buildings." Thomas pointed in the general direction in which the assassin had disappeared. He winced when, pointing with his left hand, he felt for the first time the pain of his own wound. Looking down at his left hand, he was surprised to see that it was caked with clotting blood.

Styler saw the blood at the same time. "Are you okay, Gus? Are you hurt? What happened?"

Without being instructed to do so, Kellogg, who had been listening, lifted the car radio microphone and called his dispatcher to request that an ambulance be sent to the scene. He was reminded that one was already en route for Rodriguez.

"Hey, Art, do me a favor, will you?" Thomas asked in a low voice, almost as if he was ashamed of what he was going to request.

"What's that, Gus?"

"Look, I'm not hurt badly. Let me ride back with you. Mike Rodriguez was my friend. I . . . I don't like to see him like that." He jerked his head in the direction of the corpse in the alley.

"Sure, Gus." The other detective nodded understandingly. "No sweat." He peered over at the alley and saw a pair of feet sticking out into the sidewalk. He involuntarily shuddered. There, but for the grace of God, he thought, goes any one of us.

It was while they were so engaged that another squad car pulled up, double-parking next to the first. Before the car had come to a complete stop, the passenger-side door swung open, and Lieutenant Zimmerman jumped out. He and Sergeant Donofrio, who was driving, had been working late. Since these murders had started, neither of the two men had left for home before nine any night.

Following a brief reiteration of the circumstances, and a cursory examination of the felled officer's body, Zimmerman went into action. After reminding Thomas to take possession of his partner's service revolver, which was still clutched desperately in the outstretched hand, he asked: "Which way did the man run?"

"Across the Avenue and up the street. East."

"Did he run to the north side or the south side of the street?"

"Uh, the north side," Thomas recalled.

"How did he run? Slow, fast, like a kid or somebody older?"

"Not very fast, Lieutenant. If the block had been a little longer, I think I could have caught up with him. And he had a half-block head start on me."

"Okay, Gus. You stay here and wait for the ambulance for Rodriguez.

"Styler, put your flasher on and block the far end of the next block. Bob, we'll block the near end. I don't want any traffic in or out. We're going to get this guy."

"Search the whole block, Lieutenant?" Donofrio asked.

"Nope, I think I know who our man is. We're going to walk right to his door and bring him in."

"You know who killed Rodriguez, Lieutenant?" Thomas asked incredulously. "How could you?"

"That, young fellow, is why I'm a lieutenant and you're a detective third. Of course, I'll eat those words if I'm wrong. But I don't think I am."

"Who do you think it is, Al?" Donofrio asked as they drove across the street and maneuvered into position to cut off any possibility of a car getting past them.

"I'll bet my next raise that it's Volker. Number one, he lives on this block. Number two, he's got a king-sized grudge against cops. Number three, he was just released. Number four, Rodriguez was Puerto Rican, and Volker made it very clear how he felt about them. You want any more numbers? I'll bet my next raise, he's our boy."

"You're betting more than that, Al," the sergeant cautioned. "It does seem to add up, but if we roust that guy and he didn't do it, you're going to be back pounding a beat in Brooklyn, if I know the newspapers and what they'll do to you if you're wrong."

"Bob, if I spent my time worrying about the papers, I'd never get anything done."

Leaving Sergeant Donofrio in the car, Lieutenant Zimmerman met Detective Styler in the middle of the block. Lights had gone on in windows up and down both sides of the street, and curious onlookers formed an audience anxious for a break in their day-to-day monotony.

Zimmerman led the way up the front stoop of Number 216 St. Paul's Place. They paused at the mailboxes to ascertain that Peter Volker occupied apartment 2B—second floor, rear. "Well, at least that's in our favor," Zimmerman commented. "He's got a rear apartment. He can't have seen us coming."

Styler merely grunted in reply, as the two policemen ascended the stairs and approached the suspect's door. They took up positions on either side of the heavy oak entrance, a relic of the late nineteenth century when the house was built.

Zimmerman, who stood on the right of the door, rapped his gun butt against the wood. There was no reply. He rapped again, this time commandingly. "Police officers, Volker. We know you're in there. Open up and let us in. We just want to talk to you."

"I've done enough talking to cops," came a hoarse answer.

"Volker, let us in or I'll have to break the door down. Either way, we're going to talk. Make it easy on yourself."

"No more talk," Volker shouted. "No more talk."

Before Zimmerman could say anything in reply, he reeled backward from the blast that went off inside the apartment. In the closed confines, the noise of the shotgun sounded more like a bomb going off than a gun with which one normally shoots birds. The door shook and a dozen tiny pimples rose in the wood, where the pellets nearly penetrated.

Zimmerman looked over to make sure that his brother officer was not injured, and saw that Styler was merely shaking his head in an attempt to stop the ringing in his ears. He motioned the detective to step back and allow him room to shoot the lock without danger of ricochet. Styler understood and did as he was bidden without hesitation. The lieutenant took a deep breath and fired three shots into the heavy wood. He heard a satisfying clank as the slug struck the metal lock-cylinder.

"We're coming in to get you, Volker. This is your last chance to get out in one piece. We're going to come in shooting. Open the door and throw your gun out. Then you come out with your hands on top of your head. It's the only chance you've got."

Again, both officers jumped backward at the crash of the shotgun. This time, however, no dust rose from the door. An acrid smell of burned gunpowder seemed to fill the hallway. Zimmerman and Styler looked at each other in puzzlement.

"Volker?" Zimmerman shouted. "Volker?"

But there was no reply.

Moving his free hand to the door, Styler gave it a sharp push and jumped back to the protection of the wall. The door creaked open about halfway and stopped. There was no sound from the apartment inside—just a visible cloud of gunsmoke that burned at their nostrils.

"Volker?"

Styler moved cautiously and peered into the crack. He could see nothing. He moved into the doorway, and, pistol at the ready in his right hand, shoved the door open the rest of the way with his left.

Zimmerman waited in nervous anticipation, ready to

step in and take the detective's place should the shotgun go off again.

There was no need. While Zimmerman watched, Styler became visibly relaxed. His gun hand descended to his side.

"He suicided," Styler announced.

Chapter Twenty-two   When snow falls in New York, particularly if it is the first snowfall of the season, it makes headlines in two places—New York itself, and Miami Beach. It has been postulated by some cynics that the Miami newspapers have that headline set and on the shelf, waiting—BLIZZARD BURIES NEW YORK—until they can use it.

In New York it is only the first snowfall of the season that gets this big a play in the press, unless more than a foot should actually fall later in the season. In much the same vein, however, the front page of the *Tabloid* that announces the season's first snow, was set well in advance. In this case, the layout men made it up in August, on a particularly dead news day when they had nothing better to do anyway. SNOW SWAMPS CITY, read this year's dramatic announcement. Beneath it, there was a fifteen-inch-square photograph of snowing falling in Times Square, with pedestrians scurrying in the slush. The picture had been taken two years earlier. The retoucher had only to make sure that nobody would be able to read the theater marquees; the names of the films being shown would have dated the picture.

It was with considerable disgust that the make-up men

scrapped this plate and began work on a new one. For there are certain circumstances that will drive the New York press not to run their traditional announcement of winter—the declaration of a war, the arrest of the mayor, a prominent Hollywood divorce, or a crime of such magnitude that it preempted all else. In the eyes of the editors of the *New York Daily Tabloid,* the particularly bloody slaying of Detective Miguel Rodriguez fell in that latter category.

From the *New York Daily Tabloid:*

COP SHOTGUNNED IN ST. PAUL'S SQUARE
(Story on Page 2)
SUSPECT SLAIN AFTER STREET CHASE

December 10. St. Paul's Square erupted with gunfire last night, in a dramatic pitched battle between the police and Peter Volker, previously a suspect in the Manhattan Monster murders. When the smoke cleared, Detective Miguel Rodriguez of 1129 East 111th Street, Manhattan, was dead, Detective Gustav Thomas of 16–24 Astoria Avenue, Queens, was wounded, and Volker was dead. Volker's death was apparently a suicide, according to police.

Piecing together the events that led to the gun battle, police speculate that Volker surprised Rodriguez and blasted him with a 12-gauge shotgun. Rodriguez's partner, Detective Thomas, gave chase and was wounded in the left arm when Volker turned and fired at his pursuer at point-blank range.

Badly wounded and bleeding profusely, Thomas summoned reinforcements who arrived within five minutes. In the meantime, Volker, who had not yet been identified, sought shelter in his apartment at 216 St. Paul's Place, on the next block.

Arriving on the scene, Lieutenant Alfred Zimmerman, who is in charge of the Manhattan Monster murders, immediately suspected Volker and went to his apartment.

"We knocked on the door, and warned him that we were police," Zimmerman said. "He answered us by firing his shotgun through the door. Detective Styler [Arthur Styler, of 2720 East 20th Street, Brooklyn] and I then shot the lock off and prepared to charge the suspect. Before we could do this, however, we heard the shotgun go off again. When we entered, we found that Volker had put the barrel to his head and pulled the trigger. He was dead before we reached him."

Lieutenant Zimmerman went on to comment that he was putting Detective Thomas up for a department commendation for the heroic chase he gave even though he was wounded and knew his adversary to be armed.

In a separate one-column story, headed DETECTIVE MIGUEL RODRIGUEZ, the paper chronicled Detective Rodriguez's life from his arrival in New York, to his college graduation, to his joining the police force, to his first citation (when he, as a patrolman, wounded all three fleeing thieves in a liquor-store robbery), to his nomination for the *Tabloid*-sponsored Patrolman of the Year award that same year, through his promotions, to his death. The story was liberally interspersed with quotations from his neighbors, teachers, fellow policemen, and, of course, a glowing tribute from the local ward-heeler, Antonio Perla Garcia, who claimed to have loved Rodriguez as a son (they had never met). Above the story was a picture taken of Rodriguez in uniform, on his graduation from the Police Academy. At the bottom of the story was a larger photograph, showing the detective's body, lying headless in the street.

Parallel to this, and accorded exactly the same amount of space, with a similar number of quotations attesting to his goodness, was a story about Peter Volker. The picture at the head of this column showed Volker in his conductor's uniform. At the bottom, there was a photograph of his body, not entirely headless, lying in a pool in the middle of his apartment floor.

It was not until page three that the *Tabloid* got around to telling New York, which surely could not have missed the fact, that it had snowed during the night.

Chapter Twenty-three The two policemen scarcely had finished their coffee when a new member of the staff, one Patrick Clancy, entered the room. It was hard not to smile when you saw Clancy—he looked so much the stereotyped cop. Big, brawny, freckle-faced, Clancy had been the happiest man in the department when he had been promoted, just two months ago, out of uniform to Detective Third Class. The teasing he had taken as Clancy the Cop, both from civilians and other policemen, had almost been unbearable.

"Hey, Clancy, why don't you change your name to Cohen, so people will believe you're a cop," other officers had kidded. Or, "Clancy? What kind of name is that for a cop? Anybody might think you were Irish."

In point of fact, though, Pat Clancy was a far cry from the dumb patrolman who had inspired this image at the turn of the century. He was graduated cum laude from Fordham, and had just completed law school at night. From his earliest days at the Police Academy, Clancy's superiors had marked him as a man who would go far in the department. This early impression was now backed up by the exemplary record achieved in his five years on the force.

Clancy's promotion to detective and his transfer to Homicide had been simultaneous. As soon as Zimmerman had noticed the young man's name on the list of those eligible for transfer, he knew he wanted him. He felt himself fortunate to have gotten him. And on his part, Clancy was very happy to get out of uniform and into Zimmerman's section.

Clancy was an habitual learner. He gathered knowledge, whether from textbooks or from other men's experience, as if he were a miser hoarding gold. Someday, Zimmerman knew, the young man would be a lieutenant, and would probably rise higher still. Zimmerman believed this with a confidence he felt about few men, including himself.

"What have you got, Pat?" the lieutenant asked. Clancy never bothered his superiors with anything insignificant.

"Not much, Lieutenant. We picked up the Coleman girl's pimp. His name's Owen Harris. Got him downstairs now. Do you want to question him?"

"Who's been at him so far?"

"Just me and Barnes."

A better interrogation team, Donofrio thought, could hardly be found. What Clancy's face showed in innocence, Barnes made up for in roughness. Larry Barnes, Detective First Class, had been a professional light-heavyweight fighter before joining the Department. Although he had been a Golden Gloves champion, he had never made it as a pro. Out of nine money fights, he had lost seven. In the course of this short-lived career, he had had his nose smashed into permanent disfigurement, one ear was still puffy with scar tissue, and his eyebrow ridges were thick with shiny white scars to a point where the hair grew through in shaggy patches.

His grotesque appearance, paired with Clancy's open-faced mask of innocence, made the pair an extremely effective team of questioners. While Barnes provided the terror, Clancy supplied the relief. Neither man had ever struck a prisoner, nor seriously threatened him. After an hour of gruff questioning by Barnes, who looked as if he could chew the suspect up for breakfast and spit him out, Clancy's gentleness would tend to open a man's resistance like a sluice gate. The belief they instilled was that if the suspect wouldn't talk to a nice guy like Clancy, he would be returned to the questioning of Barnes, who always seemed on the edge of losing his temper, anyway. It was the exception when Barnes got a second chance to interrogate a prisoner.

"What have you been able to get out of him?" Zimmerman asked.

"Not a thing, sir," Clancy reported as if he himself was surprised with his uncommon lack of results. "He's playing name, rank, and serial number. Now he says he wants his lawyer, too."

"Who's his lawyer?"

"He doesn't seem to have one. He says we should call the NAACP."

"He's black?" Donofrio was surprised. Somehow, the fact that Jane Coleman had been Caucasian had led him to assume that her protector and business agent would be likewise.

"Yup."

Under some circumstances, Zimmerman would have been bothered by this fact. Cries of police brutality always seemed to be given more credence in the press and the public mind when the "victim" was black. In this case, however, he was unconcerned. Detective Barnes was also a Negro.

"Do we have anything we can charge him with?" the lieutenant finally asked.

"Yeah." Clancy nodded. "After we got a make on his prints through Records, we pretty well knew that he was the guy we were looking for. He's got a record for that sort of thing." He handed a record sheet to Donofrio, listing no fewer than nine charges of procuring, Mann Act violation, grievous assault, and assault with a deadly weapon. "So we put out an APB on him. Pick up for questioning. Bill Foley in Vice recognized him in the Village last night, and sat down next to him at a bar. It didn't take the creep ten minutes to proposition Foley and offer to get him a girl—at a price, of course. Foley forked over twenty bucks, and the guy led him to an apartment that just happened to have a girl in it. Foley pulled them both in. This time we've got him on procurement, and we can make it stick. Foley made sure that the bartender, who just happened to be Sam Luden—also from Vice— saw the whole transaction. They've had that place staked out for a month. Oh, and just in case he squirms out of the procurement rap, we've got him on a better one. When we shook him down in the station house, we found six marijuana cigarettes and four packets of heroin on him. We sent them up to the lab for analysis. I think we can pretty well assume that this guy is going to spend the next few years on the State."

"You guys don't fool around, do you?" Donofrio said admiringly.

Zimmerman rose from his chair and beckoned for Donofrio to follow. "Yessir, I think we'll have a few words with Mr. Owen Harris."

Chapter Twenty-four To describe Owen Harris as surly would be an understatement. Alive with hate, his eyes radiated curses. Looking at him, Donofrio was reminded of a hunting trip he had taken, many years before. A bobcat had somehow managed to get into the cabin. They had cornered it there, spitting and yowling, hissing its combined fear and antagonism with every breath. It was the animal's eyes that had burned themselves into the sergeant's memory, overshadowing everything else. They were the eyes of the Devil himself.

"What the hell, more cops?" Harris spat as his greeting to Zimmerman and Donofrio. "What am I, some kind of animal in a zoo? Is everybody in this motherin' place going to come down here and stare at me?"

"Shut up, Harris," was Zimmerman's reply.

The two policemen were admitted to the cell by the turnkey, an ancient sergeant who had passed his point of productivity in the more demanding divisions of the Department. Donofrio leaned his body against the steel door that was closed behind them. Zimmerman seated himself on the bed.

"Come in, gentlemen." Harris postured in mock courtesy. "Make yourselves right at home. Shall I ring for tea?"

"I told you to shut up," Zimmerman commanded. "You know, you're in one hell of a lot of trouble."

"Am I, cop? I don't see how that could be. I never did

90

anything that I wouldn't recommend for my own poor old mother."

"Oh? Is your mother a whore? Is your mother a junkie?"

Before Zimmerman had finished the sentence, Harris was on top of him, forcing him down with his hands on his lapels. Spittle dripped from his clenched teeth onto the lieutenant's shirt. Donofrio gently tapped the prisoner's head with a blackjack, more as a warning than to inflict injury. "Up," Donofrio commanded. "Right now before I use this thing and put you to sleep for a while." He tapped a tiny bit harder, just enough to let Harris know he wasn't kidding.

Slowly, with great deliberation, the prisoner released his grip on Zimmerman and rose to his full stature. He was less than six feet tall, but weighed something over two hundred pounds. Very little of this seemed to be fat. He was built like a good fullback.

Donofrio waved the blackjack at him, motioning him to step back. Harris complied without a word.

"You got no call saying things like that, cop. No call at all," he finally said, while Zimmerman straightened his clothes. "Now where's my lawyer? I ain't gonna talk to no one without my lawyer. I know the law. You can't make me."

"Who's your lawyer, Harris? Give me his name and I'll put in the call myself."

"I don't know. I don't have a regular lawyer, I guess. Call the NAACP. They won't let cops like you guys persecute an innocent man like me. We got our rights too, you know. Same rights as anybody else."

"Innocent man! My God, if you're an innocent man, Al Capone must be a saint in heaven! Don't you know what you're up against, Harris? We can put you away on so many different counts, you'll spend the rest of your life on the inside. Procuring,"—Zimmerman ticked off on his fingers—"possession of narcotics, selling narcotics, grievous assault . . ."

"Wait a minute. I didn't assault anybody. What the hell are you talking about?"

"You didn't assault anybody? What about Jane Coleman? Now don't tell me! We know all about that."

"That dumb bitch told you, did she? Stupid broad. That's no assault, I was doing her a favor. She couldn't get enough of it. Believe me. If that's assault, I'm Governor Rockefeller. You couldn't make that one stick if you tried. Besides, the complaining witness ain't going to be doing any more complaining, is she? Unless she's bitching about the heat in hell!"

"What do you mean, Harris?"

"Why, she's dead. Somebody killed her. You cops know that as well as I do. What are you trying to pull, anyway?"

"We're not trying to pull anything. When was the last time you saw her, Harris? Jane Coleman."

"I thought you knew. The night before she got it. Up at her place. That's what she was complaining about. She liked a good beating with her sex. I don't know what the hell she was complaining about. She always liked it rough before. She was a . . . oh, what do you call it, someone who likes getting beat up, it gets 'em all hot and bothered . . . a, uh, masochist?"

"That's the word, all right. Masochist."

"Hey, if you guys didn't know that, you didn't know I had her the night before she got killed. Hell, she didn't complain. You guys lied to me! What do you think I am, stupid or something?"

"Yeah, we think you're stupid. We think you're a stupid ex-con who's already done two stretches on the State, and is going up for a third. This time, they aren't going to be easy on you, either."

"Ah . . . What do you think you've got? Procurement, possession? They're both short time. Two to five, maybe. That's all."

"That's not all, Harris. We've got you for selling the stuff. You had four decks of H in your pocket when you were arrested. You know what that means. You're not that stupid. One deck is simple possession—two to five. More than one is conspiracy to sell narcotics. That's a ten-to-twenty rap and you know it. And this is your third offense. You're going to draw the maximum. Man, you're going to be an old man when you get out."

"Okay," Harris sighed. He sat down on the bed and covered his face with his hands. "What do you guys want from me?"

"We want you to tell us everything you know about Jane Coleman."

"I told you already."

"Well, then, what do you know about Janet Carrington? And June Corbin? And Joanna Coldter? You help us; we'll do what we can to help you."

"Who . . . Oh, wait a minute. Just you wait a goddamn minute. Those are the other women that got themselves killed by that nut over in the park. You don't think I had anything to do with that, do you? Oh, no! You're not going to pin any of *that* on me! I don't know anything about them. I swear to God I don't."

"Don't you?"

"No sir. I sure don't. Now will you please get me a lawyer. Call the NAACP."

"I don't think he did it, Bob," Lieutenant Zimmerman said as they waited for the elevator to take them back upstairs. "I think he's telling the truth."

"I know. To tell you the truth, I don't think he killed any of the girls, either. I guess we're right back where we started."

"Not really, Bob," the lieutenant said consolingly.

"How's that?"

"Two things. First, we've eliminated another suspect . . ."

"Sure. That only leaves everybody else in the five boroughs, and the surrounding suburbs. Look, for all we know, the killer flies in to New York from Boston whenever he gets the urge to murder somebody. He doesn't even have to live around here!"

"And second," Zimmerman continued, "we got that piece of filth off the streets. The day has not been a total loss, in any event."

The two entered the elevator and ascended to their floor in silence, Debarking, they strode to the squadroom marked Homicide. Zimmerman opened the door and started to walk in, while Donofrio continued down the hall. The lieutenant stopped in his tracks, turned, and called to his partner.

"Oh, Bob?"

The sergeant turned. "Yeah, Al?"

"What you said before, about the guy flying in from someplace whenever he gets the urge to kill somebody. I was just thinking about it."

"No!" Donofrio exploded. "I am not going to check every flight in or out of New York on those days. It would take forever. Besides, he could have come in by train, too."

"Wrong. That isn't what I was going to say. What I am going to do, though, is teach you something about the detective business. Some day you may make lieutenant and have a squad of your own. If that ever happens, you'll thank me for telling you this.

"Never play all the possibilities—just the probabilities. Number one, you could never cover all the possible explanations or methods or means. You're right about that, at least—it would take forever. You have to concentrate your efforts on what *probably* happened. In this case, although it is possible that the killer came in from out of town, it's improbable. In all likelihood, he lives somewhere right in the neighborhood. The murders took place in a very small area. The only possible way to beat the horses is to play the favorites, after all. Sure, a long shot can come in, and does, every now and then. But if that's all you played, it wouldn't take you long to go broke."

"Good point, Lieutenant. Now let me ask just one question. What do you think *probably* happened in these murders?"

"I don't know, Bob," said the lieutenant as he turned and entered the squadroom. He called back over his shoulder, "After all, anything is possible."

Chapter Twenty-five   Monday, December 13, would remain in the memory of Sergeant Robert Donofrio for a long time. As inauspicious as the thirteenth of the month often is, he almost felt like celebrating. At eleven thirty that morning, he wrapped up the paperwork in which he had been drowning for the past two weeks.

After treating himself to the two-dollar blue-plate special lunch at the Italian restaurant across the street from headquarters, he asked Lieutenant Zimmerman to call a meeting of all the detectives working on the murders, with the exception of those who stood stake-out in the field. The meeting was held in the squadroom at two thirty that afternoon.

"Are we all here?" Zimmerman asked rhetorically, to begin the session. He glanced around the room, checking off faces against the names on his duty sheet. The names of the men on other assignments or on stake-out checked themselves off. "Bradley's home sick," someone called. "Got the flu, I think." Zimmerman acknowledged the communication with a nod of his head and a grunt. He had already known of the man's absence.

"Okay," he began. "As many of you already know, Bob Donofrio has been going out of his skull for the past couple of weeks trying to tie up the loose ends in the St. Paul's Square murders. No doubt, he managed to collar some of you when you were standing around the coffee machine and put you to work on it, too." He smiled. "I'm happy to say—and I know Bob is a lot happier—that the paperwork has been completed. He will be reporting to us on that.

"Now, I asked Bob to do several things. First, to check every flight between Mexico and New York, and the surrounding airports of both, for the period of the crimes. Not only did I ask him to see if Roger Carrington, the murdered woman's husband, was on any of those flights, I asked him to get every name of anybody with the same initials. Believe me, there were quite a few R. C.s on those planes, too. Now, Bob and his people were able to eliminate most of these people from the outset. Slightly less than half of them were women, for one thing. There are several names—about fifteen—still remaining. I'm going to assign these to some of you to check out with pictures of Carrington.

"Next, I asked Bob to check out a woman, one Barbara Holdakker, whom Carrington claims to have been with in Mexico. I asked him to keep that on the Q.T., and to investigate her without spooking her. It turns out that the name is a phony. At least, we think it is. We called the police in Los Angeles, where she claims to live, and they can't find anybody by that name in the entire city. So you're going to have to keep your eyes open for a twenty-three-year-old blonde with a thirty-nine-inch bust." Several of the younger detectives whistled appreciatively. "At least that was Carrington's description of her. No, Connelly, if you find her, you can't keep her." The group laughed. Connelly was the Department ladies' man.

"Third, I asked Bob to run the same kind of name and initial check on Carrington's present whereabouts. Check all the hotels. For those of you who aren't already aware of it, Carrington disappeared after leaving here. He told us that he was going to stay in his old apartment—the place where his wife was murdered—but he never showed up there. Again, the initial check yielded several possibilities. We were able to eliminate most of them in one way or another, but there are . . . in this case about fifty . . . names to be investigated. Those of you who draw this detail are going to be calling on these hotels. They range from the Plaza to semi-flophouses. Check them all.

"Now, I'll turn this show over to Bob to tell you more specifically just what he's already done, and what you guys still have to do."

While Zimmerman had been talking, Sergeant Donofrio had been circulating among the seats, distributing mimeographed lists of names. There were two lists: one, on a single sheet, the names and reported addresses of those who had taken flights that fit into the pattern; the second and much longer list, on three sheets of paper, the fifty-odd names of hotel check-ins, coupled with the names of the hotels. Donofrio finished handing out the final few copies while Zimmerman and the rest of the assembly waited. Then the sergeant walked to the blackboard at the front of the room.

"I think Lieutenant Zimmerman spelled out the job pretty well," Donofrio said. "And I'm not going to bore you with the morbid details of how we culled these names from a list that contained over three thousand names when we began this job." He smiled wryly. "It's enough to say that it was one hell of a job. I want to thank, by the way, all the people who helped.

"But we've still got a hell of a job in front of us. I don't think I really have to tell you that hotel room clerks have notoriously bad memories. Most of the time, they don't want to remember unless we make it worth their while. Well, we can't do that, as all of you should already know. If they can be made to remember, though, it's your job to see that they do. And about the worst we can threaten them with, if they're just plain uncooperative, is to bring a building inspector around. I don't think there's a build-ing or a restaurant kitchen in New York that doesn't have some sort of violation—either building code or health—in it somewhere.

"The simple fact of the matter is that we've got to turn Carrington. He's somewhere in this city, and that some-where is most *probably*"—Donofrio shot a glance at his lieutenant—"a hotel. He didn't register in his own name, and that tells us that he's hiding.

"Remember, too, that when we find him—you'll note that I say *when* and not *if*—we can't use any force to bring him in. In point of fact, we don't necessarily want to bring him in at all. We just have to know where he is, so we can keep a tag on him. There's a strong possibility that the hotel clerk will tip him off, though, so whoever does locate him will stay right there and call in. We'll get more men down to wherever it is to cover all the exits.

"While you're asking about Carrington, ask about Miss Holdakker, too. There's always the chance that they could be together—if she really exists, that is.

"Now, as far as the airlines leads are concerned, you guys are going to have to do a little traveling. Some of the addresses are in Connecticut; some are in New Jersey; a couple are upstate. You're going to go to the door, late in the evening, I'd suggest some time around nine, and tell them you're selling vacuum cleaners, or encyclopedias, or whatever you'd like. Just make sure that you have a sample and a pitch to give them just in case they'd like to buy. Under no circumstances are you to let them know that you are police. In the first place, you won't have any jurisdiction out there; secondly, we don't want Carrington getting nervous if you should happen to find him answering the door. All I want you to do is get a good look at whoever lives in the house, and report back. It's entirely possible that our boy is holing up out in the suburbs someplace. Again, if you do turn him, call in immediately. We'll get the cooperation of the local police and have the house staked out within a half hour."

Donofrio paused for breath, and looked around the room.

"That seems to sum it up pretty well. If you'll come up here when we're done I'll divide you up into teams and give you your assignments. Any questions?"

There were none.

Chapter Twenty-six   "There are two major areas in which computers will never replace good old-fashioned cops," Zimmerman said to his sergeant after the meeting broke up. "And this is one of them. You show me a machine that can apprehend and identify suspects, and I'll ask the commissioner for a dozen right now, no matter how much they cost. The other area, and maybe this is more important, I don't know, is what sent us into the building after Volker. A cop's hunch. Intuition, if you want to call it that."

"Al," Donofrio answered, "I never proposed that computers should replace cops. I thought you understood that. What I am saying is that it would make our jobs a hell of a lot easier, that's all."

"Who are we to have easy jobs? A cop's job never has been any picnic."

"Not easy; just easi*er*. Also quicker and more efficient. A computer could have saved us a week in this investigation."

"Sure, but we're still up a tree, aren't we? We know that we don't have enough information to make this case add up and point to anybody in particular. Besides, there's a pretty strong possibility that some of our facts aren't facts at all. We've questioned Carrington, Harris, Mrs. Belden, that landlady, and God knows how many other people. By the way, I sent Allen and Cooper over to talk to Mr. Coldter—they let him out of the hospital last night—and in the Corbin girl's case, we don't even have a prime suspect. Nobody seems even to have known her, really. At any rate, if one of these people was involved, you can bet your badge that he lied to us. How is your computer going to cope with that? Now, a good, well-trained cop can sometimes sense when someone isn't telling the truth. Call it intuition. Can your computer do this?"

"Only if the liar contradicts himself," Donofrio admitted. "But that still doesn't alter . . ." Before the sergeant could finish the sentence, they were interrupted by Detective First Class Ronald Moskowitz, who entered the room without knocking.

"Don't they teach you crime-lab guys to knock on doors?" Zimmerman asked sarcastically.

"You want politeness, Lieutenant? Or do you want to solve crimes?"

"What have you got, Ron?"

"If you'll just follow me up to the lab, gentlemen, perhaps we can teach you something about how to catch murderers."

This behavior was typical of the scientific investigators. There existed in Manhattan Homicide South the classic competitive rivalry between those who hunted criminals with a gun and those who did their detecting with a test tube. For the most part, it was a friendly enough situation, although on occasion, the remarks about "ghouls" were answered with cracks about "dumb cops" and a certain animosity arose.

As Zimmerman and Donofrio followed the scientist-cop to his lair, the lieutenant recalled the days when the establishment of a million-dollar crime lab was deemed as unnecessary as some now believed the purchase of the computer to be. He tried to walk the middle of the road himself—taking advantage of the value of these facilities without making them out to be the greatest thing since sliced bread, as their active proponents claimed. Still, Zimmerman was pleased that his station had one of the best labs in the business. The men who ran it and worked in it were eminently qualified—Lieutenant Abraham Holzer, who headed the lab, had a Ph.D. in chemistry from N.Y.U.; Sergeant Caruso had a master's degree in pharmacology, with a specialty in toxicology, and was working for his doctorate at Columbia at night. With the exception of a couple of the lesser technicians, the lowest qualification of any member of the staff was a B.S. degree. Their lab was so widely acknowledged as one of the best that it was frequently consulted by police departments as far away as Philadelphia and Boston. Although this service increased the workload considerably, it was a point of pride with Holzer not to turn down any of these requests.

But as much as one might admire the work of the crime lab, it was something else again to enter its confines. Despite the elaborate system of exhaust fans, the smell of the laboratory was invariably overpowering. Zimmerman was more used to it than was Donofrio, and so did not gag when they entered. The sergeant, however, involuntarily brought his handkerchief to his face.

Detective Moskowitz turned to Donofrio and smiled. "Got a cold, Sergeant?"

No answer was forthcoming.

The two men followed Moskowitz to Lieutenant Holzer's office, where Moskowitz paused and knocked elaborately at the door, smiling sweetly at Zimmerman.

"Come in," the voice of Holzer called.

Donofrio for one was glad to get into the lab chief's office. It had its own separate air-conditioning system, which ran throughout the year. The air was sweet and pure, if a little chilly, and the sergeant was able to put the handkerchief back in his pocket.

"Oh, hi Al, Sergeant," Holzer greeted them. "I think we've got something for you guys. It looks like we found the place where the Coleman girl was murdered."

"Oh?"

"Yeah. You were right about checking the basements of those buildings. We found a few things in the cellar of one-fourteen." He opened the folder on his desk. "She wasn't stabbed there, but that's where she was choked. We found a few flakes of her skin on the inside doorknob, as well as what looks like dried saliva. The saliva was also detected on a packing crate in the middle of the room, near the stairs that go up to the first floor. Also, there was dried urine and fecal material, probably hers, on the floor in the same place."

"How can you identify dried urine?" Zimmerman asked. "Bums have probably been sleeping and relieving themselves in those basements for years."

"True enough, Al. But this stuff was definitely fairly fresh. Besides, we matched it with the Coleman girl beyond any doubt. You know, that type of waste—either urine or saliva—has characteristics. It can't be typed as well as we type blood, but we can match samples. That's not all . . ."

"Why would she choose that time to take a leak?" Donofrio interrupted, before the scientist could continue.

"It was involuntary," the chemist answered. "It's characteristic of stranglings that the bladder and bowel open while it's going on. Remember, she was using all her strength to keep her breathing going. She didn't have time to worry about her voluntary muscles. And believe me, if she could have gotten away, the fact that she had fouled herself wouldn't have bothered her one bit. You read the coroner's report, didn't you? He mentioned traces of both urine and feces present in all the cases."

Donofrio recalled this detail and nodded in affirmation.

"At any rate, as I was going to say, there was something else in the urine that helped us to positively identify it as coming from Jane Coleman. *Neisseria gonorrhoeae.*"

"I beg your pardon?"

"Gonorrhea, Al. The girl, in terms you guys would understand, had the clap."

There was silence in the room as the two officers digested this bit of information.

Zimmerman finally spoke. "What do you think of the chances of the killer having caught it?"

"Well, if he had sexual relations with her, the chances are fairly good. Of course, there are some people who seem to be naturally immune, so we can't say that with any real certainty.

"There's a more important aspect to this, though. In carrying her out of the basement, even if he dragged her, there's a pretty good possibility that he got some urine on his clothes. More likely, in fact, than his having gotten blood on himself after he stabbed his victims. Remember, they were, in all but one case, dead when he used his knife on them, and wouldn't have spurted blood the way a living body would have done. But the Coleman girl's clothes were soaked through with her waste. He could hardly have avoided getting a little on himself. And it's a positive match, a definite identification, if we find it."

"Sure," said Donofrio, playing the devil's advocate. "But don't you think he would have had his clothes cleaned by now?"

"Not necessarily. I thought of that, too, and I asked Brian Collier. I had a hunch and he bore it out. If the guy you're looking for is, as Brian suspects, schizophrenic, he might well have not. Remember, he probably has one set of clothes he wears when he goes on his rampages. They're his uniform, as it were. When he's feeling sane, he probably doesn't even see these clothes in his closet. In fact, he probably doesn't keep them with the rest of his clothes at all. He only puts them on when he's his other self—the killer. In all likelihood, he takes them off as soon as he gets back home, and hides them in whatever secret place he uses—the same place he keeps this other personality. If he is schizoid, there's an excellent chance that he has never thought rationally enough about this outfit to have it cleaned. And, as I said, if we can find these clothes, we can probably make a positive identification that they were worn by the killer."

"What's the incubation period for gonorrhea, Abe?" Zimmerman inquired.

"About three days. Invariably under a week."

Zimmerman turned to Donofrio. "Check the clinics and see what cases they've treated in the time period following Coleman's death. Check the state medical society, too. Also, check all the doctors in the area. They tend to be lax about reporting these cases, so the search will have to be done in person. Take pictures of Carrington, Coldter, and Harris, and ask the doctors if any of these men were treated for it in that time period."

Donofrio sighed as he noted his latest orders in his pad. More detail work. If every doctor reported every case to a central computer, he thought, this, too, could be avoided. But in the back of his mind, even he realized how unrealistic this wish was.

"Something's bothering me, Bob," Lieutenant Zimmerman said when he and Sergeant Donofrio re-entered his office. "And I can't quite put my finger on it."

"About the Coleman case?" Donofrio asked.

"I don't think so. More about the whole thing. There's something that just doesn't seem to fit. Something that doesn't ring true. Why don't you get to work on the doctors, and I'll go through the files and see if I can figure it out."

"Will do, Chief. I'll let Goldman and Carsey check the medical societies and the report records on venereal diseases. I think I'll visit the local doctors myself."

"Feeling deskbound, Bob?"

Donofrio smiled. "Something like that, I guess."

Chapter Twenty-seven   There were fourteen doctors in the immediate vicinity of St. Paul's Square. Sergeant Donofrio knew that the odds were against him turning anything up through this line of investigation, but he also knew that he had to try anyway. His plan of attack was to see all of these doctors first, without applying any pressure, and hope for the best. If that part of the search proved fruitless, he would go to the two clinics in the area. It was, indeed, more likely that a man with a social disease would seek the anonymity of a clinic, where he could lie about his name and address. If both these paths turned up nothing, he planned to return to question the individual doctors, reminding them that he was investigating four horrible murders. He had already framed his attack—"If you want the fifth murder on your conscience, then don't cooperate."

Donofrio knew that in all likelihood, he would not be able to cross-match a patient with a suspect. But he tried anyway. Banging his head against stone walls was part of his job. Besides, the lieutenant was right. He was beginning to feel deskbound.

Thus, the sergeant was not surprised when the first eight doctors had returned the pictures to him and sworn, "None of these people has ever been treated by me, for anything." The ninth doctor, a geriatrician, had maintained that if any of his patients proved still capable of contracting such a disease, he would treat them gratis, just by way of congratulations.

The tenth doctor practiced radiology and was likewise disinclined to treat this type of malady. He hadn't seen a case, he stated, since his days as an intern.

It was the eleventh man that ended the slump. Donofrio concentrated on the doctor's face as the man riffled through the pictures, and caught a brief flicker of recognition in his eyes as he spread them out on the desk that separated them.

"You know one of these men, don't you?"

"Sergeant," Dr. Maurice Fein finally began, "I don't know quite what to do. There's a question of medical ethics, you know. I have treated one of these men; that much I know I can tell you. And it wasn't for gonorrhea. I can tell you that, too. I haven't seen a case of gonorrhea in years. We don't have too many teenagers in this neighborhood, and they're generally the ones who would bring that sort of thing to me. Their parents take their venereal diseases someplace else, where they think they can keep it more secret than they would with a general practitioner. What it is, really, is that I socialize with many of my patients. Guests in each others' homes, and all that sort of thing. I guess they feel that they wouldn't be able to look me in the face if I had treated them for something like that. Or maybe they think my wife would tell their wives,

107

somehow. Hell, my wife is the last one I'd discuss the details of a case with.

"At any rate, I did treat one of these men fairly recently. I know you'd be interested, but I don't know whether I can ethically tell you about it."

"Can't you even tell me which man it was?" Donofrio's impatience showed in his voice.

"If I did that, I might just as well tell you everything I know about him."

"Doctor, perhaps it will change your mind if I tell you that I'm investigating the murders that have taken place around here. If you shield someone, he just might be the murderer." Donofrio decided to play his trumps. "And if he kills again? You've protected your patient, but perhaps cost some girl her life."

"I assumed that was the reason for these questions. The murder investigation, that is. That's why I'm in such a quandary. It's not a simple yes-or-no decision. If I do tell you what I can, then you're going to interrogate the man, right?"

"Probably." What the hell does he think I'm going to do, kiss him? the policeman asked himself sarcastically.

"Well, frankly, I do not believe that this man would be capable of committing such crimes, and my revealing this information would, no doubt, let him in for quite a hardship. He's already had enough trouble."

"Doctor, are you a psychiatrist?" The sergeant was losing the last shreds of his temper now that he was on a scent. "Have you had any psychiatric training?"

"No. I haven't had charge of a real neuropsychiatric case since medical school. My internship, actually. I have worked with psychiatrists more recently, though."

"But you can't really judge who would be capable of what, can you?"

"No more than any ordinary man, I suppose."

"We can get a court order to make you tell us, you know. If you force us to go that route and you still don't tell us what you know, you'd be guilty of contempt of court. That could cost you your license, not to mention a jail sentence and fine."

"Don't make idle threats, Sergeant. You know perfectly well that the courts won't force a doctor to violate his oath of silence."

"I wouldn't say that, Doctor. This is a matter of murder, remember. A capital crime. I'm sure we could get the court to cooperate with the police in something like this."

"Well, be that as it may," the doctor backed up, "I don't think we'll have to go to that extreme. I'll cooperate with you, but only under certain conditions."

And about time, Donofrio thought. "What are they?"

"Well, first, I want it officially noted in whatever kind of record you keep that I only revealed this information under threat of a court order. I have to protect myself, you know."

Donofrio took out his notebook and scribbled the appropriate notation.

"Second, I want your word that this man will not be treated like a common criminal. He's a patient of mine, and I know him. He's been through quite a bit in this past month, and for a while I did think that he might have a nervous breakdown. No third degrees. No grilling. I don't know what you call it, that kind of questioning, but I want your promise that he's not going to be submitted to anything like that."

"You've got my word."

"And third, as I indicated, this is a sick man. He could have a breakdown at the drop of a wrong word. He just got out of the hospital, and it wouldn't take too much to put him back in. He's only just regaining his equilibrium. I know you have psychiatrists that work with you. I want you to arrange to have a psychiatrist present whenever he's questioned. I'm also going to insist that when the psychiatrist tells you to stop, you'll do so. You can have your psychiatrist call me, and I'll see to it that he gets the full particulars on the case, both from me and from the doctors that treated him in the hospital."

The hospital? the policeman asked himself. "I think that can be arranged."

"That's not good enough. I want your word that it will be done, and I want it noted that I insisted on all this before I would reveal my patient's identity."

"Fair enough. You have my promise." Holding himself in, Donofrio asked himself, Do you want me to sign in blood? Tell me the name!

"All right." Dr. Fein sighed and reached for the pictures that lay on his desk. He picked up one of them and handed it to Donofrio. "This man. Frederick Coldter. I treated him about a month ago for a large slash wound. It was on his left forearm. He took eighteen stitches. I took the stitches out about three weeks ago. I sincerely doubt that it has anything to do with these murders—he told me that he had an accident with a bread knife. I believe him. However, I don't suppose I'd be doing my duty as a citizen if I didn't tell you."

Somehow, the possibility that Frederick Coldter was open to suspicion in the multiple slayings had been discounted by Donofrio. The sergeant had only seen the young man once, while he was still in a state of shock at the death of his bride. The shock had seemed genuine, and Coldter's subsequent hospitalization had tended to reinforce this belief.

Now, this typical, conservative youth was elevated to

the top of the list of suspects.

If the whole reaction that Coldter had shown was merely an act, Donofrio now pondered as he left the doctor's office to return to headquarters, it was certainly an excellent one. Not only had he fooled the police; he had apparently sold the psychiatrists a bill of goods as well. It's possible, the sergeant thought, but he still couldn't really convince himself. Then again, the murderer was obviously an extremely clever man—he had eluded all efforts at detection, left no tangible clues, and had been able to commit his atrocities more or less at will, despite the cautious mood of the neighborhood and the police surveillance of the area that had been put into effect immediately after the second murder. It might just be within his powers to feign a breakdown well enough to be as convincing as Coldter had been.

Still, Donofrio thought as he pulled his car into the police garage, I'm not sure. I'm not sure at all.

Chapter Twenty-eight   Whatever it was that was bothering Lieutenant Zimmerman was still on his mind following his weekly meeting with the captain. Over the superior officer's desk was a sign reading: "Hell is where the Germans are the police, the French are the engineers, the Russians are the historians, the English are the cooks, the Italians are the soldiers, and the Americans are the lovers. If none of these offend you, leave anyway. I've got work to do."

This sign spelled out Captain Michael O'Brien's attitude in no uncertain terms. Not that he was bigoted. Just that he was a very busy man and would stand for no hemming and hawing. His individual weekly meetings with his lieutenants were dreaded affairs. Zimmerman had once described it to Donofrio as being paramilitary: "You go in, he chews your tail out for whatever you did wrong last week, you say, 'No excuse, sir,' and you leave."

The only time anybody in the Department had seen Michael O'Brien smile was when the Dodgers announced that they were leaving Brooklyn. Aside from his work and his family, the captain's only enthusiasm was the New York Yankees.

A mass murderer still on the loose after more than a month did nothing to improve O'Brien's temperament. "You bring me something concrete by this time next week," O'Brien had threatened, "or I'll take this case over myself." In that this would have amounted to Zimmerman being relieved of his command, it was a very effective threat.

But despite the unavoidable shock of the tongue-lashing he had just received, Zimmerman found that he was even more troubled by a thought that was gnawing at his memory, trying to get out.

It wasn't until he was passing Brian Collier's office on the way to his own that a glimmering of recollection came to his mind. Rapping at the door, he entered.

"Oh, hello, Al. What can I do for you?"

"I've got something on my mind, Doc, and I can't put my finger on it."

The psychiatrist grinned. "I don't do hypnotherapy on forgetful cops, you know. Only prisoners get the benefit of old Dr. Collier's magic mind reliever."

"No." Zimmerman returned the smile, slightly embarrassed. "I know it has something to do with you and these murders down on St. Paul's Square. Something you said that just isn't sitting right with the case."

"Something *I* said? What about?"

"If I could remember that, I'd remember what it was."

"Was it about Carrington? Or Volker? Or any of the suspects?"

"No, I think it was about the murderer in general." Zimmerman pondered for a moment. "Wait a minute, I've got it! Something you said would happen hasn't. Remember, you said that the maniac"—Collier shuddered at this lay description—"would kill again. He's broken his record for the amount of time between murders. He hasn't murdered anybody in over two weeks."

Zimmerman sat back in the leather chair in which he had flopped when he entered the doctor's office, and looked at Collier expectantly.

"True, Al. If he were in the classic pattern, he should have acted again before now. These guys are usually like clocks. You can usually predict when they are going to strike within twenty-four hours, if you have all the facts."

"Then why hasn't anything happened?"

"Al, you know my medical degree doesn't give me any special powers for fortunetelling. I'm not a soothsayer. I may be what you might call a headshrinker, but I'm not a witch doctor." He paused to light his pipe—a frequently used excuse of his for uninterrupted thought. "Maybe he went away. Maybe he killed someone someplace else."

"Nope. Since this thing started, I've had an M.O. circulated to every major police department in the country. There have been plenty of other rapes and plenty of other murders, but none like these."

"Well, remember that I qualified my remarks by saying that he would kill again *if* he were in the classic pattern. But each one of these cases is different. Maybe he managed to satisfy whatever was driving him to commit these brutalities."

"Do you think that's possible? Do you mean to say that he won't kill any more, period?"

"You actually sound disappointed, Al. No, it's not particularly probable. Not, that is, if he's in fact a sexual psychopath à la Jack the Ripper. He'll keep killing until he either gets caught or dies."

"What if he isn't? What if he isn't some kind of sex-crazed Jack the Ripper, as you put it? Do you think it's possible that he really wanted to kill just one of the women, and murdered all the others to throw us off the track? A red herring?"

"You like grasping for straws, don't you? Look, it's entirely possible that that's how this charmer started out. But take my word for it, the way he mutilated those bodies, he is a far cry from being sane. You may manage to have him locked away in a mental institution for the rest of his life, if you catch him, but you'll never make a murder charge stick. No matter how you cut it (pardon the pun), his actions are not those of a sane, rational man. You know the M'Naghten Rule as well as I do: A man must be capable of telling good from evil, right from wrong, at the time of his crime. Any defense attorney worth his salt could produce literally dozens of my fellow psychiatrists willing to testify that the killer could not possibly have known what he was doing. The crimes themselves almost prove this."

"In other words," Zimmerman interjected, "you're telling me that even if we prove beyond any doubt that the guy we catch committed the crimes, we'll never get a conviction. Well, couldn't he have planned the crimes this way? A sort of insurance in case he did get caught?"

"Anything is possible, Al. Sure, he could have planned

it this way. But the fact remains that plan or no, he isn't legally sane, and you'll never prove that he is."

"But doesn't the fact that he stopped prove that he's rational? That he knew what he was doing, all the time?"

"Try selling that to a jury. In the meantime, don't worry so much about your conviction. Get that guy in custody. Find him. Remember, we're only guessing, we're just supposing, that he has stopped killing people. He could murder someone tonight, and all it would prove is that we figured his timing incorrectly."

"Well, this time, at least we're ready for him." Zimmerman thought of the beefed-up stake-out force around St. Paul's Square, now eight men on duty in the area at all times. "If he does try again, we'll catch him for sure. Nobody could get through the net we've set up."

Chapter Twenty-nine   There could be nothing more impatient than two men with news to tell each other. When Donofrio walked into his lieutenant's office to communicate his findings, it was only his superior's rank that forced him to hold his tongue while Zimmerman expounded.

"I've figured out what it was that was bugging me," Zimmerman declared. "It was something that Brian Collier said. He said that the murderer would kill again, yet he hasn't. According to how we figure it—I've already talked to Collier about it—he's way overdue."

"Well, he couldn't kill if he were in a hospital bed under sedation, now could he?" Donofrio asked.

Zimmerman's eyebrows rose in a questioning arc. "What do you mean?"

"I mean Coldter. Frederick Coldter. The dead girl's much-bereaved husband. When I was talking to those local doctors, looking for a case of gonorrhea they might have treated, one of the doctors recognized him. He hadn't treated him for a venereal disease, but he did stitch up a slash wound on him about a month ago. I thought it out, and it was the same night as the first murder. The Corbin girl."

Zimmerman nodded thoughtfully. He had considered Coldter as a suspect only because he was an involved party to one of the crimes. But even in that light, the young man had only been thought of as a possibility for his own wife's assassin—not the mass murderer. The lieutenant, too, had been more or less influenced by the obvious grief he had seen at his single exposure to Frederick Coldter.

"It could be, I suppose," he said after a pause. "There are two reasons he could have stopped. One, as you say, he was in the hospital. Second, even if he could have sneaked out at night—and in all likelihood he could have, particularly last week when he was all but cured and only being held for further observation—he could have completed the job. His whole purpose in the four murders was to kill one woman—his wife. Now that he accomplished that, he doesn't have to kill any more. That would also help explain why the Coldter murder was different. He went out of his way to set up an elaborate pattern—the type of mutilation, the number of wounds—on his first three victims. He broke his stride, though, when he came to his own wife. It is possible, I would imagine, that because this was the only one of the four with whom he was emotionally involved, he couldn't be quite so methodical about it. Who knows? Maybe when the time came, he could only bring himself to stab her half as many times as the others. It does seem to fit together."

"Do you want him picked up?" Donofrio offered.

"Yeah. We certainly have to question him, in any event. Whether he did it or not."

"We've got a few problems here," Donofrio admitted. He proceeded to outline the concessions that the doctor had extracted from him before revealing his patient's identity.

Zimmerman merely nodded in affirmation, as each point was ticked off.

"Okay," the lieutenant said. "You go out and pick him up, and I'll arrange for Brian Collier to be present at all times. You'd better take the doctor's advice and handle him with kid gloves, though. I can just picture the papers telling the world that we drove some sweet, innocent kid crazy with our brutal interrogation. That would be all we need."

Donofrio rose to leave the room.

"Oh, Bob," the lieutenant called after him. "Call his boss first and explain how it's just routine questioning, and all that malarkey. After all, we wouldn't want to get Coldter in trouble, would we?"

Donofrio nodded that he would do so.

"Another thing, Bob. Did you finish checking out the gonorrhea lead?"

"No, I didn't. I came right back here when I turned this up."

"Well, get someone else on that angle, then. We can't afford to overlook anything at this point. Put Barnes and Clancy on it, if they're free."

The lieutenant thought grimly about the captain's threat.

"We can't afford to overlook anything," he repeated.

Chapter Thirty   The advertising firm of Allen, Peabody and Harding was one of the oldest and most respected in the city, as well as one of the largest. The interior décor of the lobby and private offices bespoke this image—walnut paneling and comfortable furniture designed to instill confidence in the prospective client. This is no fly-by-night johnnie-come-lately, the décor declared. Conservative to the core, Allen, Peabody was built for businessmen by businessmen. No brash young dreamers were tolerated, no matter how inspired they might be. If they ever did realize their ambitions, it would have to be somewhere else.

Sergeant Robert Donofrio glanced at the stolid surroundings while he waited for Frederick Coldter to meet him in the lobby. Nobody but clients and employees were ever permitted into the interior suites—not even policemen. The atmosphere reminded him of an English movie he had once seen, the one where the old colonel refought the Crimean War every night at the dinner table.

Several other people sat in the comfortable waiting-room, enjoying the soft upholstery, when Frederick Coldter left the inner sanctum and strode forward to face the world. He walked directly to the sergeant.

"Mr. Donofrio?" He smiled self-assuredly.

"Does it show that much?" Donofrio asked rhetorically, returning the smile and wondering how the young man had singled him out. He could see no difference between his appearance and that of at least four other men in the room.

By way of reply, Coldter merely widened his grin. "I

understand you'd like to talk to me. Would you like to use this conference room?" He gestured to a partially open door at his left, on the side of the lobby.

"No, I thought we might better talk downtown at my office," the sergeant replied.

Coldter seemed surprised, yet readily acceded to the policeman's wish.

"I'll just get my coat and hat. Beverly," he said to the receptionist, "I'll be out of the office for a while. Transfer my calls to Mr. Frees. He knows where I'll be."

"Is there any number where you can be reached, Mr. Coldter?" the professionally pretty girl asked from behind her wide desk.

"No, I don't think so. Just transfer my calls to Mr. Frees, as I said."

"Will you be back this afternoon, sir?"

Coldter glanced at Donofrio, who shrugged his shoulders in doubt.

"No, I don't think so," Coldter replied.

They rode down in the elevator in silence, and got into Donofrio's unmarked squad car, which he had left parked in a bus stop in front of the building. Neither man spoke at all until Donofrio pulled out into traffic on the F.D.R. Drive, heading downtown.

"I'd like to thank you for being so tactful back at the office, Sergeant. It doesn't do a guy's reputation any good to have the police announcing themselves to the receptionist, you know." He was referring to the fact that, per arrangement with Coldter's immediate superior Mr. Frees, Donofrio had simply asked the young lady to tell Mr. Coldter that *Mr.* Donofrio had arrived. Frees, too, was conscious of the stigma attached to a police officer calling on one of his employees—whatever the reason.

Donofrio had understood this and had complied with Mr. Frees's request, although he had to confess that it did annoy him somewhat. Thus, he merely grunted, "That's okay," in reply.

They rode for several minutes in silence before Coldter was prompted to ask, "Do you have any idea who did this terrible thing to my wife, Sergeant? I still can't get over it. We were only married for four months, you know."

"We have some ideas. We haven't arrested anyone yet, if that's what you mean."

"Oh, then I'm not going to be looking at suspects, or the line-up, or anything like that? I assumed that was why you wanted to go down to your office, instead of meeting in mine."

"No, it's you we want to talk to. Just routine, of course. We always question the close relatives of a . . . uh . . . deceased in a case like this. Quite often, you might be able to tell us, for example, if anybody else in the building or in the neighborhood might have any reason to attack your wife. Or if you saw anybody suspicious hanging around the building. That kind of thing. Remember, you went into the hospital before we had a chance to really talk to you after it happened. We've got a lot of gaps left to fill, and we hoped you might be able to help us."

"I see," Coldter replied pensively. He paused for about a minute. "How long do you think it will take? The doctors still say I should take it fairly easy for the next couple of weeks, you know. Besides, no offense, of course, but police stations depress me."

"I'll tell you a secret," Donofrio confided with a smile. "Police stations depress me, too. We'll make it as quick and easy as we can. I wouldn't plan on getting back to your office this afternoon, though. There are just so many details to wrap up that it's bound to take some time."

"Okay," Coldter said as the policeman steered the car off the highway and onto the side streets. "Let's get it over with."

Chapter Thirty-one   The stake-out around St. Paul's Square had reached staggering proportions. With eight men on patrol at all times, plus two squad cars cruising the periphery, it was unusual for policemen ever to be out of each other's sight. The constant vigil had become something of a neighborhood joke. There were so many police out there, one local wag had declared, that you couldn't walk down the street without being stopped at least twice. Beyond the jokes about cops tripping over each other, however, there was an appreciation on the part of some of the residents for what was being done for them. Mrs. Clauber in 106 had seen fit to express this by keeping a pot of coffee on the stove for them. Although they were forbidden to accept this generosity, she had made it a point to rush down with a tray bearing filled cups, whenever she saw more than one of the officers in front of her house, and insist until they finally accepted.

Although the ultimate result was discomfort—the coffee, after all, was a diuretic—they were thankful for it when it arrived. They didn't even argue with Mrs. Clauber any more. After all, it was getting into mid-December, and quite cold. After a couple of hours of moving around just to keep warm, the men found the scalding liquid a godsend.

Like an army of occupation, the police had descended upon the quiet square. And like such an army, they indulged in minor diversions to pass the time. The day after

Detective Rodriguez was killed, for example, Detective Second Class Aaron Adams and his partner, Detective Third Class Martin Faraday, had organized a massive snowball fight in the park. They both served on day watch, and faced with no fewer than two dozen neighborhood children coming from blocks away to see what they could of the previous night's battle, they decided to organize the kids into teams and stage a small snow-war. Both sides built "forts" and began to bombard each other. Soon, Adams and Faraday found themselves joining in, one on each side. Detectives Grimaldi and Horowitz took up the cry, and began pelting their fellow officers with snowballs in what amounted to a child-sized free-for-all.

When it was time for these men to be relieved, their replacements took up the battle, which didn't end until the children's mothers came to call them home for supper. It was a tossup who was more disappointed to see the game end, the children or the policemen.

For the most part, though, the stake-out detail was unutterably dull. As was characteristic of the neighborhood prior to the murders, nothing ever happened there. Seasoned veterans found themselves longing for just an hour of pounding their old beats in Times Square or the Upper West Side, where at least they were always kept occupied. It even would have made a difference if there had been some shop windows to look in, but in this residential neighborhood there were none. The people were nice enough, and tried to cooperate in whatever ways they could. Still, all twenty-four men on the round-the-clock walking-tour wished that something—anything—would happen to break the monotony.

In an atmosphere of such acute boredom, it was not surprising that when something did happen they pounced on it with glee. Thus, when on the night of December 14 a light went on in the Carrington apartment, three officers literally raced to the police phone to report. All three men had a good view of the window, and all three had apparently noticed the light at about the same time. All three had started toward the phone at a walk, then noticed the other two headed in the same direction. One broke into a trot, and the others started running for the call box. It was Detective Third Class Peter Williams, who had led Boys High School of Brooklyn to an all-city victory in track five years before, who reached the telephone first. He good-naturedly thumbed his nose at the two officers who ran up seconds later. Williams was on loan from Armed Robbery Division for the purpose of the stake-out, and took a particular pride in the fact that the two detectives he had beaten were both permanently attached to Homicide. It is always a source of satisfaction to beat a man at his own game.

"Murray," Williams said to the Communications Division officer who answered the call, "this is Pete Williams in Armed Robbery, attached to the stake-out in St. Paul's Square. Put me through to Lieutenant Zimmerman, will you?" While he waited, Williams glanced at his wristwatch. It was not yet eight o'clock, and there was a reasonably good chance that either Zimmerman or Donofrio were still in the office. Neither man, the young detective knew, had worked less than a twelve-hour day since this string of murders began. After some clicking indicating that the call was being plugged into the correct line on the switchboard, the sergeant answered.

"Homicide Division, Lieutenant Zimmerman's office. Sergeant Donofrio speaking."

"Evening, sergeant. This is Pete Williams on stake-out in St. Paul's Square. We think Carrington has returned to his apartment. There's a light on in his window, at least."

"Has anybody investigated?"

"No, Sergeant. We figured we'd better notify you first."

"Good. Let's see, D'Angelo is in charge this shift, isn't he? I'd like to talk to him."

Williams turned to the pair of Homicide detectives who stood at his side. "Hey, you guys, where's D'Angelo? The sergeant wants to talk to him."

"He should be over on the other side of the square now."

"He's around the corner right now, Sergeant," Williams said into the phone.

"Have him call me as soon as he can. You go after him yourself, Williams. I'm going to put Krauss and whoever else is there . . ."

"Carter, Sergeant."

"Okay, I'll put Krauss and Carter in front and in back of the building. I don't want him getting away from us again."

"Right, Sergeant."

"Just one more thing. If Carrington is up there, and if he does try to leave, for God's sake hold on to him. Don't arrest him, but don't let him get away. Lieutenant Zimmerman just left for home a couple of minutes ago. I'm going to try to catch him. Either he or I or both of us will be over there as soon as we can."

Chapter Thirty-two   While he was still engaged on the telephone, Sergeant Donofrio pressed the button on the lieutenant's desk that signaled whoever was out in the squadroom to come in. The signal was in the form of a flashing red light above the door, coupled with a buzzer. It had been installed for occasions just such as this, when the troops could be summoned without the lieutenant's having to interrupt what he was doing.

This night, largely because of the stake-out that had absorbed most of the available manpower, only three men entered the lieutenant's office in response to the signal.

Hanging up the telephone, Donofrio immediately ordered Detective Clancy, who had presented himself, to call the garage downstairs to see if they could catch Lieutenant Zimmerman before he left the building. Zimmerman had no two-way radio or phone in his personal car—that privilege, at the taxpayer's expense, goes to captains and above—so the sergeant instructed Detectives Barnes and O'Bannion to get their tails down to the garage. If the lieutenant was still in the building, there would be no problem and it would be a wasted trip. If, however, he had already left, Barnes and O'Bannion were to take a black-and-white car, and try to overtake him on his homeward journey and bring him back. Both had visited the lieutenant's home, and knew the route he customarily drove.

As the men scattered to their assignments, Donofrio opened the door and looked out into the squadroom. Three detectives remained, all of them engaged on the telephone, busy with other cases that were pending. No matter what might arise, even a brutal case like this current one, there was always the normal workload to be handled. The fact that a sexual psychopath was loose in the city did not stop other men from murdering their wives, or kids from sticking up liquor stores and killing the proprietors, or drunks from fracturing each other's skulls with bottles. To paraphrase, Donofrio had once caught himself thinking, Death Goes On.

125

Lieutenant Zimmerman, it turned out, had already left the building. By turning on their siren, however, Detectives Barnes and O'Bannion were able to catch up with him at the entrance ramp to the Thirty-fourth Street tunnel under the East River.

Pulling up alongside the lieutenant's four-year-old dark blue sedan, Barnes, in the passenger seat of the black and white car, waved Zimmerman over to the side of the road. Before O'Bannion had come to a complete stop in front of the car he had cut off, Barnes hopped out and trotted over to talk to his superior.

"What's up?" the lieutenant asked as he rolled down the window of his car.

"I think Carrington's back," Barnes declared. "The stake-out called in and said there was a light on in the Carrington apartment. Sergeant Donofrio sent us out to catch up with you and bring you back."

The two men stared into each other's eyes while the lieutenant digested this. Why would Carrington come back? Zimmerman asked himself. And where had he disappeared to after telling us that he was going to stay in the apartment in the first place? Nothing in this case made any sense. Particularly the actions of Roger Carrington.

His reverie was interrupted abruptly by car horns blowing behind him.

"Come on! Come on!" a cab driver, two cars behind Zimmerman's stopped vehicle, shouted. "Give the guy the ticket and stop blocking traffic. I got a living to make. It's bad enough I get stuck with a goddamn fare out to Queens!"

"Drive my car back to the station," the lieutenant instructed O'Bannion. "I'll go on to St. Paul's Square with Barnes, here."

En route, Zimmerman talked over the car radio with Donofrio, who filled him in on the details of what had happened and outlined the steps that he had initiated. The lieutenant instructed the sergeant to remain at the office. There was still the interrogation of Frederick Coldter to complete, as well as a good deal of more routine work that went on no matter what else was happening.

As the police car turned off First Avenue and drew into St. Paul's Square, Zimmerman carefully surveyed the stake-out. Three men stood in front of Number 114, where Roger Carrington lived; four more could be spotted, still patrolling the square block. Barnes pulled up in front of 106, just down the street from the house under surveillance.

Zimmerman hopped out of the car, and strode purposefully toward Paul D'Angelo, who stood on the sidewalk in front of the building, talking to Peter Williams. As he approached, Zimmerman saw that Mrs. Belden, the landlady, who occupied the first-floor front apartment, was peeking out at them from behind her curtains. He also noticed that the light in the apartment directly above—the Carrington apartment—still burned brightly.

"What's happening, Paul?" Zimmerman inquired as he drew within speaking range. "Is Carrington in there?"

"Don't know, Lieutenant. Somebody sure is. That's the first time that light's been on in weeks."

"Has anyone come or gone from the building since you noticed the light?"

"No, sir. Donofrio put Carter out back to make sure nobody got out that way, so we have all the exits covered. Not a soul."

"How did Carrington get in there, by the way? How did he get past you?"

"I couldn't tell you, Lieutenant. The only people to

even walk on the block in the past two hours were three women."

"So how did he get in?"

"Maybe the back yard, sir. Remember, we didn't have anybody back there before the light went on. Or maybe it isn't him at all. Maybe the landlady was up there, or something."

"I don't think so. We told her not to some time ago."

"If I know my landladies," D'Angelo said, "that wouldn't be enough to stop her."

"I'll tell you what, Paul. Let's go in and find out."

Chapter Thirty-three   Police interrogators are at their best when dealing with convicted felons. In this no-holds-barred environment, they are often able to extract reams of information from so-called professional criminals, without ever resorting to what the newspapers like to call the third degree. Simply enough, the professional criminal knows the game and doesn't have to be told the rules. He is well aware that the police, if he chooses to cooperate, are in an excellent position to offer reduced sentences, better treatment in the jail where he is held before trial, and other amenities that make it more attractive for him to help them than to fight.

The first time a man is interrogated in a police station, however, he is invariably innocent. An attitude of "I didn't do anything, and if you can prove that I did, I'm sorry, and in any event, I won't do it again" prevails. However surly a seasoned felon may be, he knows when he has been caught, and reacts accordingly. A first-timer, a "cherry" in the jargon of the trade, does not know where he stands, and thus maintains his innocence to the end. However many times he contradicts himself, however many proofs the police present to damn him, however guilty he may appear, he is, in his own mind, being framed. These men are invariably shocked when the jury finds them guilty, and numb when the judge passes sentence. The professional criminal is more stoical. If he is sentenced to one year in prison, when he could have gotten ten, he knows he is lucky. Such types have even been known to thank the bench for its generosity.

Questioning a man for the first time in his life is, at best, difficult. Even if he is in fact innocent, he will lie. Any fact that he believes might be at odds with the image of the self-righteous, no doubt church-going, model citizen that he is trying to sell the police, will invariably be altered. A good policeman, a thoroughly experienced interrogator, will sometimes be able to discern which of the suspect's lies are of this type—that is, the protection of his image—and which are deliberate distortions of the facts surrounding the circumstances of a crime.

A warning thought of this order ran through Donofrio's mind as he escorted Frederick Coldter to Lieutenant Zimmerman's office. The same picture always presented itself to his consciousness, dredged up from the most uncomfortable depths of his memory—the second homicide case he had ever worked on. A suspect in a felony murder, an armed robbery in which a night watchman had been slain, had persistently maintained a patently phony alibi. No matter what evidence was presented to the man to disprove his story, he continued to stick by it. It was not until the jury had actually found him guilty that he told his lawyer the truth—that he had been with his mistress at the time of the crime, and had not told the truth because he didn't want his wife to find out that he was being unfaithful. Fortunately for him, the case was reopened, and his new story proved true.

As Donofrio opened Zimmerman's door and ushered Coldter inside the office, he wondered what sort of lies this man was going to tell.

"Good afternoon, Mr. Coldter," Zimmerman began cordially. "Thank you for coming down here. And before I say anything else, I'd like to express our sympathy for your loss."

"Thank you, Lieutenant. It's very kind of you to say so."

"Before we go any further, I'd like to introduce you to Dr. Brian Collier." Zimmerman motioned toward the doctor, who was seated inconspicuously in the rear corner of the office. "Dr. Collier often works with us in these cases. He's a psychiatrist, and we've found that he can be a great deal of help to us in establishing a sort of psychological portrait of the murderer. We hope that what you can tell us about your wife's death, combined with what others have told us about the crimes in the area, will help us to learn what this man is really like, and what we can expect from him."

"I'll help you in whatever way I can, Lieutenant," Coldter offered. "But I'm afraid I really don't know very much about it. One minute my wife was alive and well; a few minutes later I found her poor body. I never saw who did it, or heard anything, or even knew anybody who might wish us ill."

"Well, I appreciate that, Mr. Coldter. But any information you can give us will be more than welcome. To start, suppose you tell us, in your own words, exactly what happened that night. From the time you got home."

"I've been through all this before with the detectives who came to the house that night, but I guess I wasn't

130

making too much sense then. Sure, here goes."

Coldter sat back in the chair and furrowed his brow in an exaggerated attempt at tapping his memory. "I arrived home a little after seven, I guess. I worked late in the office. That's easy enough to bear out—just what time I left the office, that is—we've got a time clock. It takes me a little more than a half hour to get home from there. We had a few martinis . . . No, wait a minute . . . I stopped off on my way home to pick up some Chinese food. We both work and I don't like to ask Jo to cook on weeknights." Donofrio made a mental note of Coldter's use of the present tense. "So maybe it was seven-thirty when I got to our apartment. Then we had a few martinis, and ate the food. Maybe it was the booze, maybe not, but we both started feeling hot. Jo went into the bathroom and changed into her nightgown. Then I went in and put on my pajamas. While I was in there, she told me, through the door, that she was going to take the garbage down the hall to the incinerator. She was a stickler about that sort of thing. Particularly with Chinese food. The grease, you know. It draws roaches. Whoever heard of a brand new building with roaches? But she had seen one a few weeks before, so she was extra careful about it. At any rate, she said that she was going to take out the garbage, and that's the last time I ever saw her. Alive, that is."

He paused to meditate over his last sentence, and the permanence of his loss. It was only after an extended silence that he resumed.

"It was maybe ten minutes before I came out of the bathroom. I had decided to shave. I had figured we were going right to bed."

He's blushing! Donofrio thought. He's actually blushing!

"I remember that I was surprised that I didn't see her,

and that the bed hadn't been pulled out yet. We have a convertible sofa, you know. I looked in the kitchen, and I even looked in the closet. I thought she might be playing some kind of game. Then, when I still couldn't find her, I put on my robe and went out to look in the hall. Maybe there was something wrong with the incinerator, or maybe she had stepped into a neighbor's place, or something."

"Did your wife know your neighbors? Was she in the habit of visiting them?" Zimmerman interrupted.

"No," Coldter said thoughtfully. "Or at least I don't think so. But you never know. I can remember meeting people in the hall when I had my own apartment before we got married. In fact, that's how I met Joanna. She lived down the hall from me in an apartment she shared with another girl. We met when we got off at the same floor from the elevator one night. It was funny. She had the apartment two doors down from mine. All the way at the end of the hall. When I got off the elevator at the same floor, and then when I walked the same way down the hall, she thought I was following her. She actually turned around at one point and told me to stop it or she'd call the police. Boy, was I surprised. It was only when I showed her that my apartment was right near hers that she believed me. She apologized, and I apologized, and the next thing I knew I was going over there the next night to meet her roommate and have dinner."

"Had you had any trouble with the incinerator in the past?" Zimmerman asked.

"Well, yes, actually. The chute door used to stick sometimes. Somebody on the floor used to try to put too much in at one time, I think, and the door wouldn't close all the way. Some garbage would get stuck up underneath the chute, I guess. We used to have to open and close the thing maybe a half a dozen times before it would clear. It

132

could take a couple of minutes, sometimes. I guess I figured that's what had happened, although it had never been *ten* minutes before. At any rate, to make a long story short, I went down the corridor to the incinerator, and I don't have to tell you what I found. I guess I must have started shouting, or crying, or carrying on somehow, because the next thing I knew, a neighbor—I had never seen him before—took me back to our apartment. I remember he was going to call the police, but I insisted on doing it myself. For the life of me, I don't know why." He shrugged his shoulders. "That's about all, I guess. Then the police came, and you know what happened after that."

Zimmerman watched the young man meditatively, while Dr. Collier tamped his pipe and Sergeant Donofrio scribbled quickly to complete the notes he had been taking.

"Mr. Coldter," Zimmerman finally said. "I'm sure you've already asked yourself this question a thousand times, but we'd like to ask it for the record. Is there anybody, however remote the possibility, who would have wanted to harm either you or your wife? Or is there anybody who had been paying an unusual amount of attention to your wife? Perhaps someone who made a pass at her? Anything at all that you can think of along these lines would be of help to us."

Coldter looked at the lieutenant inquiringly. "Why, no, Lieutenant. Actually that question never crossed my mind. I thought, what with all the other murders . . . what do they call him? . . . the Manhattan Maniac? . . . I just naturally assumed that he had done this thing."

"Yes, of course," Zimmerman said. "But if you can think of anybody, as I say, it would be a great help."

"Well,"—Coldter paused to contemplate this aspect— "we all have our enemies, I suppose. But certainly none that would do anything this terrible. I mean, oh, just for instance, Joanna dated a number of men before she met me. I know that one or two of them were a little upset . . . disappointed might be a better word . . . when she chose me and not them. Then, of course, she went with a fellow back in Pennsylvania for quite a long time before she came to New York. She told me all about him before we were married. As a matter of fact, he was one of the reasons she came up to New York—to get away from him, that is. You know the scene, I guess—her family liked him. They were kids together; everybody always assumed that they would get married when they grew up. Nothing very unusual about that, I suppose. But, my God! He even came to our wedding and wished us well. I'm sure he wouldn't still be bearing a grudge. In fact, I seem to recall Jo telling me that he had gotten married. Her mother told her.

"As far as people who don't like me are concerned, I suppose I have my share. Business, and all that. There was a girl I used to go with before I met Joanna, too. She was pretty upset when I told her that I wasn't going to see her any more. But, Christ, that was over a year ago. No, Lieutenant, I can't think of anybody who would actually want to do a thing like this."

"Well, if you don't mind, Mr. Coldter, we'd like the names and addresses of these people, just so that we can make sure."

"I suppose I could give you their names, as well as I remember them, Lieutenant. But I'd really just as soon you didn't make a big thing out of it with them. You know, nobody reacts too favorably to the thought that they're suspected of murder. Besides, I'd just as soon they didn't start calling me and accusing me of telling the police that they killed my wife."

"Don't worry, Mr. Coldter. It won't be anything like that. All we want to do is verify where they were when the murder took place. I have absolutely no doubt that most of them will be immediately above suspicion."

"Well, all right," Coldter agreed, and dictated a list of about a half-dozen names to Sergeant Donofrio. The sergeant handed the list to the lieutenant, who opened a desk drawer and put it aside.

"Ouch!" Zimmerman exclaimed as he slid the drawer shut. He shook his hand in the air in front of him, as if to cool it. "Damn, I caught my hand in the drawer. Oh, that hurts!" It was a convincing enough performance to draw the attention of Dr. Collier, who began to rise to look at the injured hand.

"No, that's all right, Doctor. I'll be okay. Just clumsy, I guess." Zimmerman caught the doctor's eye and held it. "Now," his look said, "keep your eyes open because I'm going to make my move."

"That reminds me, Fred . . . you don't mind if I call you Fred, do you?"

"Actually, I've always disliked the name. My friends call me 'Rick.'"

"Rick, then . . . when you were in the hospital, the doctors noticed a fresh scar on your left arm. Did you have an accident, too?"

The question had taken Coldter off guard, and the surprise showed in his face. For a moment he just looked at Zimmerman, as if trying to fathom the purpose of the question. All he saw was a man waving a stinging hand in front of him, alternately massaging the meaty side that had been pinched in the desk drawer. Coldter smiled.

"As a matter of fact, I did. About a month ago, I guess. Maybe it was six weeks. Frankly, I don't remember that well. To tell you the truth, I did an awfully dumb thing.

It was that damned incinerator. It was stuck, as I said sometimes happened, and I put my hand down to see if I could get whatever was blocking it up. That chute has pretty sharp edges on the inside. Well, I freed the door and the chute swung up and caught my arm." He pulled back the sleeve of his jacket and unbuttoned his shirt cuff. About three inches up the arm from his wristwatch was a long pink scar, running across the back of his forearm. It stood out plainly against the freckled skin.

"That's quite a cut," Zimmerman remarked.

"Yes," Coldter replied. "I bled like a stuck pig."

"I'm sure you did."

Zimmerman looked at Donofrio, who had been trying to catch his eye to remind him, without words, that this was not the same story that Coldter had told Dr. Fein. Zimmerman had already realized this, and merely nodded his acknowledgment.

"Mr. Coldter," Zimmerman resumed, "if you wouldn't mind, I'd like to have a couple of my men escort you home. They'd like to search your apartment. Perhaps we can find some clue as to the murderer's identity. You know, maybe Mrs. Coldter knew somebody that you didn't know about. Maybe she had a fight with one of the neighbors that she forgot to tell you about. Also, we'd like to talk to the man who helped you home after . . . after you found your wife's body. Perhaps he saw or heard something. Do you remember his name, by the way?"

"No, Lieutenant, I don't. Why didn't you ask him your questions when you first came to our place? The night the crime took place?"

"Because he wasn't there, Mr. Coldter. You were alone in your apartment when the police arrived."

Coldter looked shocked. "He wasn't there? But . . ."

"Well, perhaps you can pick him out from among your

neighbors. My men will help you."

"If you insist, Lieutenant. Although I'm sure you won't find anything in our apartment. My wife didn't keep any secrets from me, you know."

"Did Mrs. Coldter keep a diary? A lot of girls do, you know."

"Yes, I think she did."

"Did you ever read it?"

"Of course not!"

"Well then, we've got something to look for, don't we? Sergeant Donofrio will see you home now. All right?"

Chapter Thirty-four   There are many kinds of silence, and very few are as void as the word itself would seem to imply. There is a silence when a husband and wife are at home reading, a peaceful quiet; and there is the silence of the subway train, when the high noise-level precludes conversation. There is the silence of prayer at a funeral, a silence charged with grief. And then there is a special silence, the loudest of all, when a man is sunk so deep in his thoughts that, although he feels he should be engaging in conversation and making small talk, he cannot. He knows that something is going on around him, he even suspects what it is, yet he is afraid to open his mouth for fear of making things worse. His thoughts are all of figuring out exactly what is happening, and his place in it. And how, if he feels himself to be implicated, he can wriggle free without making matters worse by the very act of trying.

It was this last type of silence that pervaded the unmarked police-car as they rode from the police station

back to St. Paul's Square and the home of Frederick Coldter. Driving the car was Detective Third Class Patrick
Clancy. Seated next to him was Coldter, and in the back
seat, legs awkwardly stretched to fit around the equipment
that customarily is found in the back seats of police cars,
was Sergeant Robert Donofrio.

The silence was heavy and oppressive. More and more,
Coldter felt that he must say something, just to break this
evil spell. Preferably something light and humorous. A
man who has so recently lost his wife, his bride in fact,
should not feel particularly funny, and he feared doing
this, lest a harmless joke make him seem callous.

"Sergeant," Coldter finally inquired, turning in the seat
and resting his arm on the backrest, "do you people actually suspect that I had anything to do with my wife's
death?" Better to get the whole thing out in the open,
where it could be dealt with as a fact, not a suspicion.

Donofrio smiled. "Officially, Rick, my answer has to be
Yes. But we suspect a lot of people." The sergeant
reached forward and took Coldter's arm in as friendly a
fashion as he could muster. "Unofficially, of course, I
don't think so. As I said when we left your office, this is
largely a matter of routine. I'll tell you a secret—the vast
majority of murders are committed by husbands and wives
upon each other. So, you see, it's only natural that we
have to keep you on the official list of possibilities. We
wouldn't be doing our job if we did otherwise. However,
I don't think you had anything to do with it, just between
us."

"Maybe, if that's the case, I shouldn't have agreed to let
you search the apartment," Coldter ventured with a wry
smile.

"Why not? You don't have anything to hide, do you?
Besides, you know as well as we do that we could always

138

get a search warrant.

"Look, if we're lucky, we may find something that will clear you entirely. Maybe in your wife's diary. All sorts of strange things have been known to happen in these cases. For all we know, the elevator operator has been making advances to the girls in the building. Maybe he's some kind of nut."

"Self-service elevators," Coldter informed him.

"Well then, the doorman perhaps."

"Perhaps."

The car eased up to the curb in front of The Hawthorne. The doorman started to come to tell them that they couldn't park there—that it was a building entrance —but recognized Clancy as one of the detectives who had visited the building to investigate Mrs. Coldter's death, and returned to his post. As they got out of the car and walked to the entrance to the apartment house, Coldter looked at the doorman with cold suspicion as they passed him. The man's blank expression was devoid of any emotion or answer.

Together, the three men strode to the elevator, which took them to the sixth floor.

As Coldter opened the apartment door with his key, Donofrio spoke. "A couple of other detectives—from our crime lab—will be stopping by in a few minutes. Just to look for fingerprints; that sort of thing. I hope you don't mind."

Coldter looked up as he finished turning the key, before he swung the door open, as if to say, "Would it do any good if I did mind?" "No, of course not," he said. "Let them search away."

Coldter and Clancy entered the room, while Donofrio stood outside. "Rick," Donofrio called him back. "Why don't you and I look for that man while Detective Clancy looks through your apartment? Perhaps we can save a little time."

Coldter shrugged his shoulders and stepped back out of the apartment. Clancy stayed inside and began his search while Coldter accompanied Donofrio to the opposite end of the hall. When they reached the incinerator, Coldter stopped. "This is where . . ." he began. He had started to tremble, and Donofrio reminded himself of the warning that Dr. Fein had given him.

"I know," Donofrio cut him off. "Which apartment did the man who helped you come from?"

"I'm not sure. This one, I think." He indicated the door immediately to the left as they faced the incinerator closet. Without hesitation, the sergeant walked up to it and knocked.

"Yes? Who is it?" a woman's voice called.

"I'm a police officer, ma'am. We were hoping you might be able to help us."

The tiny peephole, shielded by a mirror on the outside, clicked open.

"Could I see your badge, or some identification?" the woman requested nervously.

"Of course," Donofrio answered. He took out his wallet and held the badge up near the peephole.

"Without looking," the woman's voice demanded, "what is your badge number?"

"One-o-four-seventy-one," Donofrio recited.

"One-o-four-seventy-one," the woman repeated, reading the stamping on the badge. The peephole snapped shut and the lock clicked open and the door opened a crack. It was held securely with a chain. "What do you want?" she asked cautiously.

"Ma'am," Donofrio began, "do you recognize this gentleman standing with me?"

She strained to see, but the inch that the door was open would not permit her to do so. After much trying, she finally made up her mind and closed the door, removed the chain, and reopened the door wide. A frumpy little matron, she stood in the doorway in a bathrobe, her feet encased in enormous furry slippers. She stared at Coldter inquiringly, then asked, "Isn't he the young fellow down the hall? The one whose wife . . . ?"

"Yes, ma'am. This is Mr. Coldter. Did you see him on the night his wife was killed? Mr. Coldter says that some gentleman in one of these apartments was kind enough to assist him that night, and he'd like to thank him personally."

"Young man," she addressed Donofrio. "I have been a widow for three years. I'm not in the habit of having male visitors at that hour of the night. I can assure you that the man you are looking for did not come from this apartment."

"I see," said Donofrio calmly. "Did you hear anything that night, ma'am? Anything unusual out in the hall?"

"No. With the noise those girls make upstairs from me with their carrying on until all hours of the night, it's a miracle I can hear anything at all."

"Oh? Was there a party upstairs that night?"

"No. I wouldn't call it a party. They always carry on like that. Honestly, how they expect to find nice husbands when they play around that way is just beyond me." She visually appraised Coldter. "But then, I imagine the young men today are no better. Honestly, I remember when I was a girl, young ladies . . ."

Donofrio cut her off. "Thank you very much, ma'am. We won't trouble you any further. Be sure to keep your door locked. You're wise to check everybody who wants to come in."

The woman was obviously miffed at having been cut short in her discourse. After staring dumbly at the sergeant for a moment, she shut the door hard. As they turned away, they could hear the chain clicking back into place.

"Well, maybe it was this apartment." Coldter indicated the door to the right of the incinerator closet. He quickly corrected himself when he got a better look. A sign reading EXIT was emblazoned across the door. "Hm. Must be a staircase. Funny, I never noticed that before." He turned and looked at Donofrio. "You don't think . . . ?"

"I don't know. Let's try the other apartments before we start jumping to conclusions."

The next two apartments yielded similar results. Frightened tenants, behind bolted and chained doors, knowing nothing. Nobody heard anything; nobody saw anything; and let's just leave it that way, shall we?

They were about to knock on the fourth apartment door when Clancy called from the opposite end of the hall. "Oh, Sergeant! I think you'd better come here and see something."

Automatically, they started to move down the hall, back toward the Coldter apartment. Before they had gotten ten feet, though, the door opened on the first apartment they had visited.

"Young man," the woman called. "Policeman. I want you to do something for me before you leave."

"Yes, ma'am?"

"I want you to go upstairs and tell those girls to quiet down. They're at it again. That phonograph of theirs is blaring away, and it sounds like they've got a parade going on. Honestly!"

"Yes, ma'am. I'll stop off up there before I leave."

They walked away abruptly, leaving her standing in the

doorway.

"Honestly!" they heard her exclaim. "These young people today just have no manners at all. None at all."

They did not hear her door slam until they had reached the Coldter apartment. Detective Clancy stood at the open door waiting. There was something large and formless in his hand.

"I found this in Mrs. Coldter's dresser drawer, Sergeant," he announced, handing the bundle to Donofrio. The sergeant accepted it and unfolded it until he could see that it was a man's white shirt. The left arm and front of the shirt were covered with a crusty red-black stain.

"This, too, Sergeant." The detective held up a man's tan raincoat, slightly worse for wear; the collar and cuffs were beginning to fray. It, too, was stained with what almost certainly was blood. "I found this stuffed under the same dresser."

Coldter had entered the apartment and sat down on the couch while the policemen spoke quietly in the doorway. When they walked toward him, he glanced up at them. His face showed noticeable signs of shocked surprise when he saw what they were carrying.

"Oh, boy," he mumbled, and braced himself for their questions.

Donofrio spoke first, holding out the garments in either hand. "Coldter, have you ever seen these before? This shirt and this raincoat?" A new gruff tone had entered the sergeant's voice.

"No, I don't think I have," Coldter answered after studying the garments.

"Oh, come on, Coldter. Detective Clancy found them stuffed under the dresser in the bathroom. Your wife's dresser."

"Well, maybe they are mine. I'm not sure."

143

"You're not sure?" Donofrio fairly shouted. "My God, man! Either this is your raincoat or it isn't."

"Well, maybe it is," he admitted.

"And I suppose you never saw these stains before! And I'm sure you have no idea whatever how they got there."

"I didn't say that. Stop trying to make me look stupid, will you? They're mine all right. I got those stains on them when I cut myself on the incinerator door. I told you I bled a lot."

"You wore your raincoat to take out the garbage?"

"Yes, I don't have a bathrobe."

"But you wouldn't have needed a bathrobe, if you were wearing your shirt and pants!" He shoved the shirt forward until it was less than six inches from the suspect's nose.

"No. I didn't have the shirt on. Just my pajama bottoms. I never wear tops. The blood dripped on the shirt back in the apartment. I guess I had just thrown it on the bathroom floor, and I bled on it." He stopped to collect his thoughts. "Jo always said I was a slob when it came to my clothes."

"Coldter," Donofrio demanded, "take a good look at this shirt. A good look."

The sergeant held out the sleeve. Under the blood stain, the shirt had been cut. "Do you still say that you bled on it, and not through it?"

"Yes."

"Mr. Coldter, I think you'd better come back downtown with us. We are going to book you on a charge of suspicion of murder. It is my duty to inform you that anything you say may be taken down in evidence and used against you. You are entitled to legal counsel. If you cannot afford a lawyer, we will ask the court to appoint one for you before you are asked any further questions. Do you understand that?"

There was a stunned silence by way of reply.

"Do you understand, Mr. Coldter?" Donofrio asked more gently.

"Ye-e-e-s, I suppose so. But why are you doing this? Believe me, as God is my witness, I never killed anybody."

"That remains to be seen, Mr. Coldter. There is ample evidence for us to suspect that you did."

"Evidence? What evidence? That shirt? The raincoat? Believe me, that's *my* blood on them. Your lab will show that. It's my own blood. I never killed anybody."

"If that were all there was, I wouldn't be taking you in. The fact is, Coldter,"—Donofrio's voice hardened again —"that you have lied to us. We have caught you in your lie. That, plus the actual physical evidence of blood-stained clothes, is more than enough for me to arrest you on suspicion."

"Lied to you? What lie have I told? I haven't lied to you!" Coldter shouted.

"You know what lies you've told us, Coldter. Why don't you tell us which statements you made weren't true? It will be a lot easier that way, believe me."

"But you can't arrest me. I haven't done anything."

"You lied, didn't you?"

"Well . . . No, I didn't. I've only told you the truth. I wish to God you'd tell me what it is that I'm supposed to have lied about."

"Perhaps we will, Coldter. Downtown at the station."

Chapter Thirty-five   D'Angelo and Zimmerman looked at each other, the detective as if to say "Now, Coach?" The lieutenant nodded, and they began ascending the stairs in front of the brownstone. It was only when they reached the inside glass door that their progress was halted. The door was on a buzzer system, and locked. Without speaking, Zimmerman leaned across and rang the first bell, that of Mrs. Belden, the landlady. It took less than thirty seconds for the woman to appear and admit them to the inner confines of the building.

"Mrs. Belden," the lieutenant inquired, "were you up in the Carrington apartment tonight?"

"Why, no, Lieutenant. I haven't been up there since you told me not to. What makes you ask?"

"There's a light on up there. Right now."

"Hm, I thought I heard noises. But it can't be Mr. Carrington. Once you heard his footsteps up there, you'd never forget what they sound like. That man never learned to walk quietly. Sounded like a herd of elephants, all the time he lived here."

The two policemen looked at each other quizzically.

"Thanks for letting us in, Mrs. Belden," the lieutenant said as they mounted the staircase. She started to follow, and D'Angelo turned and advised her to return to her apartment. "We don't know who's up there, Mrs. Belden. I think you'll be safer in your own place." She looked at Zimmerman, who nodded his agreement. "Well, all right," she conceded reluctantly. "But please try not to wreck the place. I've got enough troubles."

Reaching the door, the policemen stationed themselves on either side and drew their pistols. D'Angelo knocked. "Police officers. Please open the door." Memories of shotguns coursed through Zimmerman's brain, causing him to shudder involuntarily and draw closer to the protection of the wall.

But no guns went off. Before D'Angelo had to call a second time, the door swung open. A girl stood in the

146

doorway—a very attractive girl.

"May we come in?" D'Angelo asked.

"May I see some identification?" she asked, staring at the revolver the detective was still holding at the ready.

"Certainly," Zimmerman answered, producing his badge.

She opened the door the rest of the way and admitted the two policemen, who in turn returned their sidearms to their holsters. D'Angelo made a quick search of the apartment, while Zimmerman merely stood staring at the young lady. However immune he may have become through two years spent with the Vice Squad on his way up the police chain of command, he was still not beyond being affected by a woman this attractive. From her small feet through her tightly trousered legs, through her narrow waist, up to her remarkable bust, her thin, long neck, and her innocent—almost angelic—face, she was as close as he had ever seen to how a red-blooded American boy thought a woman should be assembled. Her long brown hair flowed around her shoulders in a careless abandon that must have taken her an hour in front of a mirror to achieve. She wore little make-up, but the lipstick and scant touch of power had been applied with the skill of a woman who knows that she is beautiful. In another day, they would have said that the lieutenant was smitten.

"Yes, officer?" she inquired of Zimmerman, smiling at the knowledge that whatever business he might have here, he had paused to observe her beauty. "What is it you want?"

The lieutenant's mind consciously shifted out of whatever gear it was in, and returned to business. It was not without will power that Zimmerman managed to accomplish this. From the recesses of his mental filing system, a hunch emerged.

147

"Miss Holdakker?" he asked.

She smiled again. "Why yes. How did you know?"

"Lucky guess. Miss Holdakker, what are you doing here?"

"Why shouldn't I be here? Roger—Mr. Carrington, that is—said I could use this apartment while I'm in New York. Is there any reason why I can't? It is his apartment, isn't it?"

"Yes, you've got the right place, all right. When did you last see Mr. Carrington, though?"

"Oh, a few weeks ago, I suppose. In Acapulco. He gave me the key and said that I could stay here. I told him then that I expected to be in New York around now. Actually, I'm a little surprised not to find him here. They're casting a play I'm interested in, and I flew up for the auditions. I'm an actress, you know."

"I never would have guessed. You haven't seen Mr. Carrington since you left Mexico? You're sure?"

"Of course I'm sure," she replied, a trifle nervously. "Is anything the matter? Where is Roger, anyway?"

"That's what we were hoping you could tell us, Miss Holdakker. We've been looking for him for some time now."

"Is anything wrong? He's all right, isn't he? Nothing's happened to him, has it?"

"No, we don't know of anything that has happened to him, Miss Holdakker. We'd just like to know where he is. We have to ask him some questions."

Zimmerman thought quickly, and decided to resolve another mystery while he was at it. "Miss Holdakker, I'm sure you wondered how I knew your name. Well, to tell you the truth, we've been looking for you, too. Mr. Carrington told us about you—I must say, his description didn't do you justice—and when we couldn't locate him, we thought we might be able to find you."

"Well, here I am." She smiled.

"Yes. So you are. Miss Holdakker, Roger Carrington told us that you came from Los Angeles. In our search for you, we naturally checked with the police department out there. They couldn't find anyone of your name, or any record of anyone of your name. Could you explain that, do you think?"

She furrowed her brow, as if to indicate that she didn't care for the idea of policemen looking for her and checking into her background.

"Well, of course they didn't have any record of me. I've never been arrested."

"I'm sorry. You misunderstand. Every city has a postal directory with the name and some address for everybody who gets mail. But the Los Angeles police couldn't find your name. Also, they checked with Actors' Equity, Screen Actors Guild, Screen Extras Guild, all the usual sources. Nobody ever heard of Barbara Holdakker. We sort of wondered why not."

"You don't have to rub it in, you know. So I never made a film. Not even as an extra. And I never appeared in a play, outside of Des Moines, that is. That doesn't mean that I'm not an actress."

"Sorry again. I didn't mean it that way. But how come the post office has no record of you? Surely, you've received mail."

"Under my old name." She made a face. "I changed my name when I came to Hollywood. A lot of girls do, you know. Men, too. Did you know that Tony Curtis was really Bernard Schwartz? Now what kind of romantic actor has a name like Bernard Schwartz?"

"What was your old name, Miss Holdakker?"

"Why? You're not going to check back in Des Moines,

are you? That's all my parents need—the police asking about me."

"Don't worry about that. We aren't going to bother your parents. All we'll do is check the Hall of Records in Iowa to verify your story."

"Well, okay, I guess. My real name, as you put it, or at least the name I was born with, is Julia Barbara Choldenheimer. C-H-O-L-D-E-N-H-E-I-M-E-R. That's some name for an actress, isn't it? God, with a name like that they'd cast me as some kind of fat German hausfrau. Can't you just picture that on a marquee? Julia Choldenheimer? No, I'll be Barbara Holdakker, if you don't mind."

"Fair enough, Miss Holdakker. You'll get no argument from me. Now just one more favor. If you do happen to see Mr. Carrington, would you please *not* tell him that you talked to us and that we were looking for him? Also, if you do see him, would you please call us as soon as you can?" He handed her his card.

"Certainly, Lieutenant," she answered after reading the card. "But why can't I tell him that you want to see him, so he can contact you?"

"We'd really prefer it our way, Miss Holdakker, if you don't mind. Just call us when you see him, please."

"Sure."

D'Angelo returned to the living room from the bedroom, where he had been searching—for what, he didn't know. "Nothing, Lieutenant," he announced.

"Okay," Zimmerman said. "Let's be on our way."

"Oh, Lieutenant," the girl called after him as they descended the stairs, "it is all right if I stay here, isn't it? I mean, there's nothing wrong here, is there?"

"It's all right with us," Zimmerman answered. "There's nothing at all wrong, unless you count the fact that Carrington's wife was murdered in that bedroom. If it doesn't bother you, it doesn't bother us."

As they came down the front stoop, the lieutenant turned to D'Angelo.

"Paul, I want you to stay on this. Call your guys together and describe this Holdakker girl. I want the front and back of this building covered at all times. If she leaves, I want her followed. And don't be fooled by the color of her hair. She dyed it once, and she can change it again."

"How do you know she dyed it, Lieutenant?"

"When we interrogated him, Carrington described her as a blonde. Now her hair's dark brown. That may be its natural color—probably is—but we can't be too careful. I don't want her to get away from us. It's your job to see that she doesn't."

"Yes *sir*," D'Angelo responded, unaccustomed to hearing his superior officer using such a strong tone of voice. "Don't worry about a thing."

Zimmerman merely nodded as if to say, "I hope so," as he got into the car and instructed Detective Clancy to drive back to the office.

"I may not get home tonight," he commented as they drove along. "One of these fine days I'm going to requisition a couch for my office. If I have to stay there twenty-four hours a day, I might as well be comfortable."

Chapter Thirty-six   It is the most basic of human traits to complain. Most people never grow out of this habit. Po-

licemen, even detectives, are no exception. Deskbound for
the majority of their working days, the troops that now as-
saulted the field in search of Roger Carrington, using as
their treasure maps the names and addresses furnished by
Sergeant Donofrio, were nevertheless complaining bitterly
within a few hours. However much this assignment came
as a counterpoint to their workaday jobs, however much
they might have wished to get outside last May, few were
happy with their new task. It had soon become apparent
that their job would not be an easy one. Stop after stop,
question after question, they had all drawn blanks. Nobody recognized the pictures. At three of the houses, the
people insisted that they had never heard of the name
given by the airline, even though the address matched.
One of the addresses turned out to be a shopping center.
After questioning each shopowner and manager individu-
ally, the detectives had still not gleaned a single kernel as
to the whereabouts of Roger Carrington.

Two by two the teams reported back to Manhattan
Homicide South, the men hangdog and tired. Defeat
lined their faces like maps of the areas they had combed.
Most of the men had not been content simply to check the
houses on the airline list; they had tripled and quadru-
pled their work by adding houses next door and houses
with similar numbers. Thus, if 21 Cedar Drive had been
one of the addresses on the initial list, they had also investigated at 12 Cedar Drive, 121 Cedar Drive, and 21, 12,
and 121 Cedar Road, some three miles away. Still, they
had found nothing.

Those detectives who had been assigned to the hotel detail had fared, if possible, even worse than the househun-
ters. Not only had they not managed to come up with
even the slimmest lead; they did not even believe that
they could eliminate the places that they had checked.

The hotel detectives themselves, in the inns that had them, were worse than useless. They constituted, in fact, quite a hindrance. Not only did they refuse to cooperate with the detectives, they were also knowledgeable enough to assert that the police couldn't force them to help. Most were disgruntled ex-policemen themselves, who had either been fired from, or in the better cases, retired from the city's police force. The men who had been dismissed from the public trust wouldn't have thrown the detectives a rope if they were drowning; the retirees insisted on bending their ears for as long as they would listen, talking about the old days.

The investigating officers could not eliminate any of the places they had visited because they knew that room clerks lied, elevator operators lied, and hotel detectives lied. The first two lied for anyone who would slip them five dollars. The last might mislead the police just for the fun of it.

The only hope that these officers had was that they might stumble upon Carrington by accident. The chance of this happening, they knew, was slim.

It was no surprise to any of them that they came back to the station house empty-handed.

"Okay, gentlemen," Donofrio began when they had all seated themselves in the room where they had been given their assignments. He looked around him and saw legs sprawled in the aisles, collars unbuttoned, and neckties askew. "You've all reported in now, and I thought you'd like to hear the results. According to you gentlemen, Roger Carrington doesn't even exist. In the whole city of New York—in all five buroughs, not to mention six suburban counties—this man is a figment of Lieutenant Zimmerman's imagination. Well, let me tell you something. Despite what you may be thinking, the lieutenant isn't the only one who saw him. I did, too. Yes, Virginia, there is a Roger Carrington.

"How'd you like to hear what your assignments are going to be tomorrow?" Donofrio teased. "Well, I'll tell you what they're going to be, and I'm sure you're just going to love them." Donofrio proceeded to read a list of eight men who had been on house detail—the men who had not bothered to extend their investigations to similarly numbered houses. "You gentlemen are going to take over hotel detail tomorrow. Compare notes with the men who had that assignment today, because they are going out into the suburbs tomorrow instead of you, to cover the ground that you missed. In addition, the following men"—he read off four more names—"will form two teams and cover any possible error on the four houses where either the resident never heard of the passenger's name or the house doesn't exist. Not just numbers, either. They're easy to transpose, but so are names of streets. Example—" he pulled an address seemingly at random. "Take this one. Two twenty-one Sutton Street. Now if you check in Manhattan, you'll find a Sutton Place, a Sutton Place South; in the Bronx, there's a Sutton Parkway, and a Sutton Park Road; in Queens, there's a Sutton Boulevard, a Sutton Crescent, a Sutton Street, a Sutton Road, and an apartment house called The Sutton. Now let's say you investigate all these and still come up empty. What do you do then? I'll tell you what you do then. You look in your city guide. The book with all the street maps? In the index, if you bother to look, you'll find that there is also a Sutter Street in Brooklyn, as well as several other similar street names. Now I don't expect you guys to come back here tomorrow empty. If you haven't turned this Carrington by tomorrow night, you'd better have some damn good reasons why not."

Donofrio paused to catch his breath. Again, he scanned his audience, noting a dull hostility in its eyes. It was as if the men were telling him, "We'd love nothing better than to knock the crap out of you for the way you're driving us, but we can't be bothered to get off our tails and try."

"Those of you who haven't been reassigned, report for stake-out duty on St. Paul's Square on your regular shift tomorrow. Check at the lieutenant's office. A roster will be posted there within a half hour. Those guys haven't had a day off since this case started. They can use some relief from you well-rested guys." A harsh, sarcastic laugh arose in the room as Donofrio turned his back on the assembly and left through the door in the front of the room.

If there's anything at all in this line of approach, we should know tomorrow, he told himself as he walked back to his own desk. He didn't want to think about what they would do if there wasn't.

Chapter Thirty-seven   When a man who has been lying decides, at long last, to tell the truth, there is no stopping him. The words burst forth in a flood tide of absolution and guilt, fear and exhaustion. For this reason detectives, particularly those who have had experience with the art of interrogation, can almost always tell when a man is, in fact, telling the truth. It is not what he says and how much sense it may or may not make; it is the way he says it.

So it was with Frederick Coldter.

Donofrio had escorted the young man down to the first vacant cell in the lockup—right next to the drunk tank. Wordlessly, he saw him locked in by the uniformed sergeant in charge of the jail section. "I'm going upstairs to book this one, Charley," he said as he turned away from Coldter. "Suspicion of murder." "Hey," Charley had responded, right on cue. "That's a bad one. Too bad. Looks like a nice kid." "Nice kids don't kill people," Donofrio answered, and left the area.

It was four hours before he returned. Four hours in which Frederick Coldter sat alone in his cell. Time for him to watch the parade of alcoholics and vagrants, petty thieves and wife-beaters pass in front of the bars that confined him. Four hours with an aching bladder. There did not seem to be anyplace where he could relieve himself. He tried to see what the other men were doing, but he couldn't make it out. There was a shallow basin on the floor of the cell, but he wasn't at all sure that that might not be his food bowl. If it was, he certainly didn't want to foul it.

It was some time before he got up the courage to call the guard. "Officer, could I speak to you when you get a chance?" he called after the man as he passed, escorting another limp alcoholic into his nightly haven. The policeman looked up in surprise at the manner of the request. On his way back to his desk at the end of the corridor, he deliberately did not stop at Coldter's cell.

It was about twenty minutes later that Sergeant Donofrio returned. Coldter was surprised that he found himself feeling glad to see him.

"Look," he implored. "I really don't know what you want from me. No doubt, it's some kind of misunderstanding. Tell me where I'm supposed to have lied, and I'll straighten it out. Please!"

"Booking sheets." Donofrio held up a sheaf of papers in his right hand and seated himself on the cot, relaxing.

"Look, Sergeant." Coldter squirmed. "Isn't there some

156

kind of bathroom around here?"

"Use that pan." Donofrio indicated it.

Coldter looked at it in disbelief. He had read of such things in nineteenth-century novels but would have scoffed if he had been told that there were places in the United States of America, in New York City, in fact, that relied on this type of plumbing. "Maybe later," he finally said.

Donofrio had been studying the young man closely. He had contradicted himself, yet Donofrio couldn't avoid the feeling that Coldter was not their man. Still, feelings weren't enough.

"Rick," he offered, "I'm going to do you a favor. I think you're a nice kid who has gotten himself confused. I'm giving you the benefit of the doubt as to why you lied. Now, for one thing, you claim that a man helped you back into your apartment. Yet we can't find any such man. We called at the apartments he could have come from, yet we can't find him. Do you have any explanation for that?"

"We didn't go to *all* the apartments. There was one left."

"Clancy stopped there before he came back here to-night. After the crime-lab guys arrived. While we were waiting downstairs in the car for him. It's occupied by two elderly folks. A retired couple, in fact. They didn't hear anything that night—they both wear hearing aids, any-way. And the man certainly isn't the one who you say helped you. Boy Scouts help *them* across the street; they don't do the helping."

"Well, there was an exit door there. Remember? Maybe he came from there."

"Nope. Couldn't have. Have you ever used one of those emergency exits, Rick?"

Coldter shook his head in the negative.

"They're one-way doors. You can get into the stairwell from any floor, but you can only get out on the ground floor. The fire law says that the building has to have such a staircase for emergencies, but if people could exit any floor, all sorts of burglaries would be taking place. The outside door is never allowed to be locked, remember. Anyone can get in. In any event, your Mr. Helpful didn't come through there."

"Well, I swear to you that there was such a man. I don't know where he came from. I said I wasn't sure which apartment it was. I said I had never seen him before. I'm telling you the truth. I can't prove it, but I am."

"Okay, then let's let that question alone for the moment. There's a much more important area in which you've lied."

"What's that?"

"How did you get that cut on your arm? The scar?"

Coldter did not reply at first. Then he declared, "I told you. I caught it in the incinerator chute. I told you that before."

"You told *us* that story before, but you told other people something else, didn't you?"

"What do you mean? That's what happened. I caught my arm in the incinerator."

"Then why did you tell Dr. Fein that you cut it with a bread knife?"

Coldter recoiled as if he had been struck across the face. He moved backward at the force of the verbal onslaught.

"I didn't . . ."

"Oh, come on, Coldter. It's too late to lie now. I'm trying to see things your way. I'm trying to be on your side. But I can't if you tell me one thing and other people another. See, I'm not accusing you of a thing. Just tell me the truth about how you cut your arm."

"It was in the incinerator," he tried one more time. "It just seemed too stupid to admit it to the doctor."

"I won't buy that, Coldter. You're an intelligent fellow. If you had cut yourself in a garbage disposal area, surely you would have asked the doctor for a tetanus shot. You would at least have told him where it happened, so he'd know to look for infection. No, Coldter, Dr. Fein described the wound, and your scar matches. Clean, straight —that cut was made with a knife. It's a slash wound. I'm no doctor, but I've seen enough of those to know. Now how did you get it?"

"Okay," he sighed. His shoulders slumped in resignation. "My wife did it," he declared in a small, yet emphatic voice that led Donofrio to believe he just might be telling the truth. "We had a fight about a month before she died. We were both pretty drunk, I guess. Well, one thing led to another, and I slapped her face. She picked up the bread knife and swung it at me. I put my arm in front of my face to defend myself, and she cut it. She saw what she had done, and immediately stopped fighting. I didn't want to go to the doctor, but she insisted."

He paused, searching Donofrio's face for some sign of belief.

"That's the God's honest truth. I swear it is."

Sergeant Donofrio was honestly puzzled when he went back upstairs. He tended to believe the young man, but this new story, if anything, incriminated him more. It was, he conceded to himself, an ample excuse for the lie. If the police were looking for a knife-slayer, you are not going to tell them your wife attacked you with a knife. It would lead to only one conclusion, after she was found stabbed to death. Also, it accounted for the lie to the doctor.

Donofrio made a mental note to inform Dr. Collier of his turn, and have Coldter transferred to a better cell. It looked as if the young man would be with them for a while. At the moment, he was the A-number-one most likely suspect.

Chapter Thirty-eight   "Robert Cameron, 1252 East 30th Street, Brooklyn; Randolf Carter, 1851 Park Slope Terrace, Brooklyn; Robert Cohen, 9 Maple Drive, Scarsdale; Mr. and Mrs. Raymond Culligan, 31 Bryant Drive, Syosset," Donofrio read to the lieutenant. "In none of these four instances do the names match the addresses. The one in Syosset turns out to be a shopping center; in the others, people of different names live at those addresses. They never heard of our names, either. We checked all similar addresses and likewise drew a blank. We even went so far as to check the Post Office Directory. There are seven Robert Camerons listed, no Randolf Carters, one hundred nine Robert Cohens, and fourteen Raymond Culligans. Not one of them has an address that even remotely resembles the ones we were given. We ran a quick check on all of them anyway. Only one out of the one hundred thirty was even out of town during the period in question. A Robert Cohen. He was in Miami Beach. We checked it out and it jibes.

"All the other people on the list that the airlines furnished were where they said they were. But none of them are Carrington."

"Okay," Zimmerman said. "Good job, Bob."

"Good job? We didn't learn anything, did we?"

"I should say we did. By the way, did the airline verify that Carrington flew up here when he said he did?"

"Yes. We expected that, didn't we?"

160

"Uh huh," the lieutenant affirmed. "I want you to get back to that airline—which was it, Pan American?"

"That's right."

"And check another set of initials. See if there were any women on the flight with the initials J.C."

"J.C.? As in the victims?"

"Yup, I've got a hunch."

"You want to let us mortals in on it?"

"Not yet. I'm not that sure of it myself. It's only a hunch. You check that out with Pan American. It should only take a few minutes. It's only one flight, this time. And this time, if a girl with those initials was on the plane, see if the airline will give you the names of the stewardesses on the flight. We'll want to talk to them."

"Sure, Al," Donofrio agreed. "I wish you'd tell me what's going on, though."

"I will soon enough, Bob. Don't worry about it."

"Right or wrong?" Donofrio asked, grinning.

"Right or wrong." Zimmerman smiled back.

Chapter Thirty-nine   The door had no sooner closed behind Sergeant Donofrio when the lieutenant's telephone rang.

"Homicide, Lieutenant Zimmerman speaking," he answered.

"Oh, Lieutenant. I'm glad you're still there. This is Barrett, on the St. Paul's Square stake-out."

"Yes, Harry. I'm not glad I'm still here. I haven't seen my wife in days. Now what's on your mind?"

"That Holdakker girl. The one who was in the Carrington apartment. She's leaving. D'Angelo's on her tail. He passed me and told me to call you for instructions."

"Okay, Harry. Without making a fuss, catch up with D'Angelo. Pick up another man on your way. The two of you take his place. She's seen him before, and she might recognize him. I'll radio the unmarked car in the area and ask them to join the tail, too. Whoever you get to assist you, don't walk together. Split up. We don't want to spook her. I don't care how many men you need for the job; don't lose her! Now get going."

The phone clicked in Zimmerman's ear and went dead as the young detective took up his new task.

"Now things are starting to happen," Zimmerman said out loud to no one in particular. His mind went back to the tongue-lashing the captain had given him, and the ultimatum. "We might just beat your deadline, sir," he mumbled. "We might just do that little thing."

"Were you talking to me?" Donofrio asked as he re-entered the room.

Zimmerman looked up with a start. "No, Bob. This case must be getting to me. I was talking to myself." He shook his head as if to clear it. "What did you find out?"

"Well, I don't know how you knew it, but you were right. There was a girl with the initials J.C. on that plane. Julia Clifford. What's more, the airline had a record of the seating arrangement. She sat right next to Carrington."

"Good, good. What about the stewardesses?"

"Pan Am is checking. They know who the two girls were who had charge of that cabin—first class—but it's going to take a few minutes for them to find out where they are now. Apparently the girls just go into a pool when they finish a run. They could have been assigned anywhere."

"Hmm. Well, when they call back, I want you to check something else with them. Who was that husband and wife on the list of phony passengers?"

"Umm, Mr. and Mrs. Raymond Culligan."

"Was that a Pan Am flight, too?"

"Yes, it was."

"Get the names of the stewardesses. I have a feeling that Raymond Culligan and Roger Carrington are the same man."

"What about Mrs. Culligan?"

"I think our dear Miss Holdakker, who changes her names and her hair color with about the same regularity, might just fill that bill."

Recognition came into Donofrio's eyes. "Oh, so that's what you've been driving at," he declared. "These phony names and addresses. You think they're all Carrington!"

"It could be, Bob. It could very well be. What's more, I'm willing to bet that if you compared the dates of those flights with the times of the murders, you'll find that they match. Without even looking, I'll bet that each was roughly one day before the corresponding murder."

Donofrio took the list from his jacket pocket and studied it. He glanced up at the blackboard four times, to compare the dates on the list with those, written in chalk, for the murders.

"They all match except the last, Al."

"That makes sense. The Coldter girl's murder was only two days after the Carrington woman's. He didn't have to fly back for that."

"Wait a minute. Then you now think that they were all done by the same man? I've got Frederick Coldter locked up downstairs, remember."

"I know. I'm not saying positively that he didn't kill his wife, either. So we'll hang on to him for a while yet." Zimmerman paused thoughtfully. "Wait a minute. The flight that doesn't match. Which was it?"

Donofrio consulted the list again. "That was Robert Cameron. He flew from New York to El Paso on November twenty-second. Round-trip ticket. The other half of the ticket hasn't been used yet." Donofrio looked up. "That's pretty unusual in itself, you know. That's the divorce flight. Down to El Paso, go over to Juarez the next morning, and come back to New York on the noon flight the next day. Some people stick around for a while, but not many."

"Sure, sure." Zimmerman thought out loud. "Carrington had to get back down to Mexico so he could fly back up here from Acapulco a few days later."

"Have you had any feedback from the hotel down there?"

"Not yet, Lieutenant. They're pretty slow about things down there, I guess. You know, *mañana?* I'll see if we can't goose them up a little." He made a note to call the hotel himself, the next morning.

"Well, Roberto, I'll bet you a cup of coffee that they tell us that Carrington was there all the time. But, of course, like so many other tourists down there, he went out big-game fishing occasionally—for two or three days at a stretch."

"Lieutenant," Donofrio declared in mock despair, "I already owe you enough cups of coffee to keep you awake for the next eight years."

"Well," Zimmerman yawned, then glanced at his wristwatch, "why don't you get some of that coffee now. It's already eleven-thirty, and there's no sign that we're going to get home at all tonight."

Chapter Forty   Barbara Holdakker, also known as Julia Barbara Choldenheimer, also known as Julia Clifford, had indeed spotted Detective D'Angelo when he started to follow her away from the Carrington apartment. She had expected it. What she had not expected, however, was that she would lose him so easily. It seemed too easy. Suspicious that she had, in fact, been picked up by another escort, she decided to make her route as devious as she could.

Her first step along these lines was to head for the Astor Place subway station. On the way, she saw that two men were heading in the same direction. She went around one block completely to make sure. They followed her. With cool determination, she progressed through the turnstile and down to the platform level of the station. It was deserted at that hour, as she had known it would be. A single bum slept on a bench on the downtown side. She went back up the stairs and passed through a corridor that led to the uptown track. As she had suspected, the police would not follow her into a deserted subway station. They couldn't, without allowing her to get a good look at them and tipping their hand.

What she did not know was that, anticipating this move on her part, the police had beaten her to the punch. The "bum" was an officer who had arrived roughly two minutes earlier, rushed to the spot by an unmarked squad car. Detectives had been similarly dispatched to the next stations, both northbound and southbound. Likewise, she had no way of knowing that the frumpy woman with her hair in curlers, carrying a shopping bag, who joined her to wait for an uptown train, was a policewoman. The woman moved to within ten feet of her, but there was nothing unusual in this. Lone women on subway platforms at night did tend to draw close to each other for protection. Nor was there anything out of the ordinary about the fact that the woman boarded the same car and sat opposite her.

Moving northward, Miss Holdakker-Choldenheimer-Clifford looked at the other passengers as they boarded, but did not identify several of them as members of the police force. No fewer than six of them were. She had no way at all of knowing that by the time she reached Forty-second Street and disembarked, along with several other people from the train, every northbound station on the route was populated with at least two police officers. The man who pushed past her when she changed to the shuttle train was one of them. When she boarded the Seventh Avenue express heading downtown, she had no way of suspecting that the nun who sat opposite her had a snub-nosed .38-caliber Police Special revolver carefully tucked into her habit. She started for a moment when the uniformed Transit Authority patrolman walked into the car, but rested easier when he continued through to the next car without so much as glancing at her. She had spotted the TA lapel-pin and reasoned that he only worked the trains, and was not following her. About that much, at least, she was right.

When she got off the train with everyone else at Flatbush Avenue, the last stop in Brooklyn, she did not look twice at the people who followed her to the taxi stand. It was, after all, after midnight—almost one o'clock, in fact—by then. Nobody was going to take a long walk home at that hour on those deserted streets on a cold night, and the buses ran infrequently.

Again, she became mildly suspicious when she noticed that a car was following her cab, and got out three blocks from her destination. She peered into it as it passed, and breathed easier when she saw that it was another cab, carrying the same nun who was on the train. There was, after all, a convent only a few blocks further on.

As she walked the quiet, residential streets, the only other person she saw, in all the three blocks, was a man walking a dog—a large German shepherd. She dismissed this entirely. She could not have known that the man was Detective First Class Howard Alter, out of Brooklyn Homicide South, who had been rousted from his bed and told to hit the street less than one minute after the nun in the taxi had used the "cab's" radio to call her position to the squad car that lurked two blocks away.

She had no reason to suspect, when she ascended a short stoop and put her key in the lock of the front door, that she had been tracked to her lair, just as well as if she had escorted the police there by the hand.

Less than five minutes after she closed the door behind her, there were four policemen surveying the house, but she had no way of knowing this and less reason to suspect it.

Chapter Forty-one   There are some times when, Gilbert and Sullivan to the contrary, a policeman's lot *is* a merry one. These days are few, and the times of tedium are many, to be sure, but they do help to make it all worthwhile.

Despite the late-night grogginess that infected the

squadroom at Manhattan Homicide South, despite the short tempers that lack of sleep can produce, despite the all-pervading wish that it would all be over, this was one of those nights.

Neither Donofrio nor Lieutenant Zimmerman had slept in over twenty hours. Then it had only been for about an hour and a half. Yet they both perked up to peak efficiency when the reports of the tail on Barbara Holdakker started to come in. It was like watching a war from a command post, Donofrio had thought. Though he knew that his feet were dragging as he walked, and though he knew that he was operating on sheer nervous energy, he wished himself out in the field where the action was.

When, at one twenty A.M., the report came in that the house had been located and the stake-out, the four-man surveillance team, had been set up, both policemen burst into broad grins.

"We've got him, Al," Donofrio declared jubilantly. "We've got him."

Zimmerman, only slightly calmer, said: "You're assuming, of course, that Carrington is in there."

Donofrio looked shocked. "But he is, isn't he? He has to be."

"Don't worry. I'm pretty sure he is," Zimmerman said. "He'd better be, with the runaround that girl gave us. You know, I'm beginning to see what the British used to like about fox hunting. It can be quite a bit of fun, as long as you're not the fox."

"I suppose so. I never looked at it that way. By the way, now that we've cornered the fox, how are we going to catch him?"

"What do you mean?"

"Well, we could go in right now and bring him in, but you seem to want to wait. The stake-out, and everything."

168

"Yeah, I did give that some thought. But it's easier to take a man on the street. If we want to go into his home, we'll have to get a search warrant and a separate warrant for his arrest. Remember, although the circumstantial evidence is piling up—enough to make us think that Carrington *is* our man—we don't really have enough yet to make a murder charge stick."

"Well, for Christ's sake," Donofrio exclaimed, "we can pick him up for anything. Vagrancy, if need be. Once we've got him, we can grill him to our hearts' content. We'll make him talk."

"And what happens if we don't? We can hold him on a vag for forty-eight hours, seventy-two at the most. He's been playing it pretty cute so far. If we have to let him go again after we've got him, it will queer the whole thing. We've got to have a charge of some sort so that we can hold him for a while, not just a couple of days. In the meantime, we've got enough men on the stake-out in Brooklyn to follow the girl, him, should he decide to go for a walk, and still keep an eye on the house."

"I don't see why we can't just pick him up on suspicion of murder. We can hold him indefinitely on that."

"True, Bob. But the magic word in this case is evidence. Okay, we've managed to establish that he *could* have committed the crimes. And he's certainly behaved suspiciously enough to tell us that he *might* be our man, but we still don't have one iota of proof that he *did* murder those girls. The district attorney would throw us out of his office if we brought him a case like that."

"I suppose you're right," a deflated Donofrio conceded. "But how are we going to nail it down? He could stay in that house for years. He could pull the model citizen routine for the rest of his life. Then what are we supposed to do?"

"Remember what I told you about possibilities and probabilities, Bob? Sure, he could go through the rest of his life without making a mistake. It isn't impossible. But remember, this is a man who has already killed four women. I don't think he's going to dawdle away the days playing Boy Scout. Sooner or later, he's going to foul up. And when he does, we'll be right there, waiting.

"I don't expect him to do anything else tonight. He's probably asleep in bed by now." Zimmerman looked at his watch again. "Any sensible man would be. Tomorrow, I'm going to instruct the stake-out detail to pick him up for anything for which we can hold him for thirty days or more. Right now, I'm going to find myself an empty cell and try to get some sleep. You may not realize it, but our shift starts in only six hours."

Donofrio looked at his own watch and grimaced. "I've still got some work to do, Al. Some woman just turned up at the Nineteenth Precinct and told the desk sergeant that she killed her husband. They're sending her down here."

"Why here? The Nineteenth isn't in our half of this town. Send her up to Homicide North."

"Too true, but she lives on Fifteenth Street. That makes it our bailiwick. Seems she decided to take a ride up town to see a movie after she killed him. One of those theatres up on Fifty-ninth Street, I guess. She watched the movie through twice, and started looking for the nearest police station. That's the Nineteenth. She's on her way down here now in a patrol car."

"Well, I guess we're lucky they didn't tell her to take the subway. You take care of it, will you? It sounds pretty routine. If I don't get some sleep soon, I'm going to collapse. I'm dead on my feet as it is. The lock-up sergeant will know where I am."

Chapter Forty-two   Sergeant Donofrio was awakened the next morning by Larry Behrens, one of the newer technicians from the crime lab. As was his custom in the lieutenant's absence, Donofrio, as second in command, had taken his superior's desk. In addition to the privacy of the office, as opposed to the bullpen atmosphere of the squadroom, it had the advantage of a telephone with several extensions. With two stake-outs in the field, and all sorts of officers calling in, this was particularly useful.

In this office, Donofrio had overseen the booking and initial interrogation of the woman who had slain her husband. A pathetic creature—classic pug-nosed Irish good looks gone to seed in the great American tradition of fat and forty—she could not tell them why she had done it. All she recalled was standing there afterward with the bloody vegetable knife in her hand. Dr. Collier had once described this type of crime as a "murder of menopause." Change of life can alter women's minds as well as their bodies.

Donofrio's decision had been to lock her up in the psychiatric section and place her at the head of Dr. Collier's list in the morning. After they had left, the sergeant had placed his feet up on the desk and began to read the morning paper. He could not recall falling asleep in that position, but that was exactly how Behrens found him at eight-thirty the following morning.

"Hey, Sergeant," the technician greeted him. "Your wife thrown you out of the house?"

Donofrio awoke with a start. He almost fell over backwards, the newspaper falling from his chest to the floor, and his legs nearly paralyzed from spending the night in an awkward position. Carefully, he lowered his feet to the floor, feeling the tingling sensation as the blood rushed back into them. He stamped a few times, to get himself going again. Finally, he rubbed his eyes and looked up.

"Oh, hello, Behrens. What can I do for you?"

"It's not what you can do for me," the technician crowed, "it's what I can do for you."

"Well, while you're being so charitable, why don't you run down the hall and get me a cup of coffee? Black, no sugar."

The technician was nonplussed. He had only been with the department for seven months, and it was impossible for him to tell when the regular detectives were kidding or not. He could tell, however, that this sergeant did need some coffee, so he turned and started to leave the room.

"Wait a minute, kid," Donofrio called. "Leave those papers you've got here, and . . ."—he fumbled in his pocket for change—". . . get yourself a cup, too."

The sergeant's eyes were still so bleary that he could scarcely read the scientific log sheets. They seemed to have something to do with blood. He pushed the papers back across the desk, as the young man returned, carrying a cup of steaming coffee in each hand.

Donofrio accepted the nickel change from the quarter he had given Behrens. After swallowing the first scalding gulp of coffee, the sergeant found his eyes focusing once more.

"What have you got?" he asked, mustering his best second-in-command voice. If he had tried that with any of the detectives who knew him, they would have laughed. Behrens, however, was still young enough and rookie enough to be impressed.

"These are the reports on the bloodstains on the clothing you brought in last night, sir."

"I can see that, Behrens. You're the scientists. I'm not going to wade through all this mumbo-jumbo. What do the reports say?"

"Well, sir. The blood on the clothing—both the shirt and the raincoat—is type O positive. The commonest kind of blood, sir."

"Does it match the suspect's blood type."

"Yes, sir, it does. But it also matches that of two of the murder victims."

"But you couldn't positively say that it did not come from the suspect."

"No, sir. I couldn't. It might very well be his own blood. Is that his story?"

"Let me worry about what his story is, Behrens. Did you find anything else?"

"No sir, not to speak of. We found quite a few latent prints. We've already identified most as belonging to either the suspect or his wife. There are still a couple we haven't matched up yet."

"Call me when you do," Donofrio ordered.

"Yes, sir." Behrens replied automatically. He escaped from the office as quickly as he could without actually running. "We'll tell you as soon as we know more," he called through the door.

"You do that," Donofrio muttered. "You just do that."

After the door closed and the sergeant was alone once more, he promised himself that he would have to take the kid to lunch one of these days when he had a chance. He hadn't really meant to be quite that gruff. It just came out that way.

It was eight-forty, he realized, as the morning shift of

detectives started to drift in, the night trick leaving. Picking up the phone, he dialed the internal four-digit number for the lockup. "Sergeant," he announced to the guard who answered the phone, "this is Donofrio in Homicide. Let my lieutenant go." As he hung up, he wondered whether they would be releasing Frederick Coldter today, too.

Chapter Forty-three   "No," Zimmerman said emphatically, speaking loudly over the drone of his electric razor. "We certainly are not going to let Coldter go today. Just because one piece of evidence can be explained away does not mean that he didn't do it."

"No it doesn't," Donofrio agreed as he waited his turn for the use of the lieutenant's razor. "But it sure helps a defense lawyer establish reasonable doubt."

"Not if we don't use it as evidence, it doesn't. Remember, the murder of Mrs. Coldter was still characteristically different from the others. He could very well be our man, even if it's just on that one."

"But last night you said that you thought Carrington did them *all.* Don't tell me you changed your mind again."

"I haven't changed my mind one bit. I still think that Carrington murdered all four women. It all fits for him to have done it. As far as Coldter is concerned . . ."—he clicked off the razor, its hum slowly tapering to silence—". . . let's just say I'm hedging my bets. A bird in the hand, and all that. There's still plenty to point to the fact that he did kill his wife. Certainly enough to hold him on suspicion. Plus, we've already got him. We wouldn't want

174

to let him go just to have to pick him up again. Besides, I've got a hunch he can help us. Frankly, I'm not at all sure how, but I think we're going to be glad we held on to him."

The lieutenant handed Donofrio the razor. The sergeant, taking his place in front of the small mirror that was nailed to the closet door in anticipation of just such all-night stands, spun the starter wheel. It took three tries before the motor engaged and set up its clamor.

"I suppose you want to bet a cup of coffee on it," Donofrio suggested.

"If you'd like," Zimmerman agreed.

The telephone rang and the lieutenant leaned forward to answer it.

"Homicide, Lieutenant Zimmerman. Yeah, wait a minute, will you?" Covering the mouthpiece with his right palm, Zimmerman called to the sergeant, "Shut that damn razor off, will you. I can't hear myself think." Donofrio complied quickly. "Yeah, Cooper." Zimmerman returned to the telephone. "He left? Do you have a good make on him? It's definitely Carrington. Good. Yeah, I'll get Communications Division on it. Don't sweat it. Just don't lose him. Who's on it? Oh, good man. I'll get a couple of unmarked cars out to assist. No, don't pick him up unless he does something. And I don't mean spitting on the sidewalk. I want at least thirty days with that guy. Just follow him and see what he does. Keep in touch with us back here. Good. Bye.

"Carrington just left the house," Zimmerman announced. "Get ahold of Communications and tell them to send a couple of cars over to help with the tail; no black-and-whites, either. Unmarked cars. Then get ahold of Lieutenant Hanna at Brooklyn South Homicide and let him know what's going on. Tell him we can use any men they can spare for this tail. We can't let him shake us."

"Hanna's got his hands full himself, you know, Lieutenant. It was in last night's paper. Two bodies found in a parked car in Canarsie. The style was Mafia but the victims were just a couple of kids out necking," the sergeant informed his superior.

"Well, just tell him that whatever he can spare will be appreciated. Christ, we've done those guys enough favors, haven't we?"

Donofrio put the electric razor back in its case and returned it to its hiding place. As he crossed the room, he stroked his still well-stubbled chin and thought, I guess I won't get to shave at all today.

Chapter Forty-four   In the movies, and on the spy series on television, the good guys invariably lose the men who are following them. This is a source of great amusement to the men who follow people as a part of their normal work. It is almost impossible to accomplish this feat, unless, of course, you know you are being followed.

It seemed evident to Detective Second Class Barry Molina that Carrington was not possessed of such foreknowledge. The man was making absolutely no effort to shake the detective, and Molina thought, if this were a hoodlum, he would have suspected that he was being led into a trap. It was almost too easy. Carrington had walked to the corner, turned right, crossed Bedford Avenue, and continued to head toward Nostrand Avenue. Molina had followed half a block behind on the other side of the street. At Nostrand Avenue, Carrington had stopped at the bus stop on the corner and waited. Without a second thought,

Molina crossed the street and joined him in waiting for the bus. The policeman realized that this put him in a bad position, but he really didn't have very much choice. If, for example, Carrington had decided to leave the bus stop, Molina could not have done likewise without jeopardizing his cover. The pursued, in other words, can change his mind about anything he wants to, but it would be too much of a coincidence for the pursuer to follow suit without tipping off his prey.

As he walked up to the bus stop and took a position about six feet behind Carrington, Molina was relieved to spot an unmarked prowl car across the street. If Carrington did decide to head in the opposite direction, the car would discharge one of its two occupants, who would take up the surveillance.

This was not, however, the case. After about a ten-minute wait, both men boarded a bus headed away from Manhattan, toward the bay. The bus only had a few passengers in it, and—fortunately, Molina thought—Carrington did not head for the very rear. Instead, he sat in the fifth seat, opposite the vehicle's rear door. The detective, however, did go to the last seat. Through the back window, he saw the prowl car make a U-turn as the bus pulled away from the stop. As Molina watched, he saw the detective in the passenger's seat use the two-way radio to signal headquarters of the direction of the pursuit. Before the bus had made four more stops, Molina saw another car join the procession.

The problems would start, Molina knew, when Carrington disembarked. Again, he could not follow without arousing suspicion. While he watched, the first police car on the scene jockeyed up into position in front of the bus, effectively bracketing the conveyance. When the bus stopped to pick up or discharge passengers, the detective knew, this car would keep going. It would circle the block and come up again from the rear. Then the second car would pass and play the same game. When Carrington got off, he would still be covered by one of the cars, if not both.

All very methodical. All very effective. All very thorough.

The one thing that neither the detective on the bus nor those four men in the following cars had anticipated was that Carrington would stay on to the end of the line. In this case, that meant Marine Park, one of New York City's largest, yet least used, recreation areas. By this time, Carrington and Molina were the only two passengers on the bus, and it was with some trepidation that the detective disembarked. Carrington had made it a point to use the bus's front door, while Molina exited through the side. This was a deliberate effort on the part of the detective to throw off any suspicion. It seemed to have worked.

When the bus pulled away, again giving Molina a clear field of vision, he spotted Carrington about two hundred yards ahead of him, on the opposite side of the street. He was walking quickly on one of the concrete paths that cut diagonally across the park, leading to the baseball and football fields. Since it was mid-December, the park was deserted.

Before crossing the street himself, Molina caught the eye of one of the men in the prowl cars. The man lifted his hands palms upward, as if to say, "What do you want me to do? We can't drive through the park." Molina, using hand signals, indicated that he wanted the detective in the car to follow on foot, using another path some five hundred yards back in the direction from which they had just come. The man nodded and left the warmth of the police car, thrusting himself forward into the bitter wind that blew, unchecked, across the park's flat expanse.

Molina took the same walkway that Carrington had used.

It was not difficult to keep up with Carrington—at a safe distance, of course—but it meant abandoning any pretense of secrecy. Nobody would be going for a walk in the park on a day like this. There was no question in Molina's mind that if Carrington turned and saw him, he would know that he was being followed. There could not have been any other explanation of his presence.

A sudden gust of wind blew the powdery snow that lay on either side of the walk into the air in a blinding swirl. Molina shut his eyes and put his hands in front of his face against it. When it had settled again, he could no longer see Carrington.

Disregarding the icy concrete, he broke into a run. The guy had to be here somewhere. He dashed to the approximate point at which Carrington had stood when he last saw him, but there was no sign of the man. Ahead approximately twenty yards lay the point where three paths intersected. Molina could see the other detective trudging toward him, about six hundred yards back on the branch to the left. The path to the right was partially obscured by trees. The continuation of the course he had been following was clear, but empty. Molina turned to the right.

"Officer?" a voice called from behind a huge maple behind him. Molina stopped still. "You are a policeman, aren't you?" the voice asked.

"Yes I am," Molina finally replied after what seemed an hour.

"You've been following me for days, haven't you?" the voice demanded. "No! Don't turn around!" it ordered when Molina made a move to do so. "You're not going to follow me any more!" the voice announced. The next thing Molina knew, there were gloved hands around his neck, squeezing. Crushing.

In a backward lunge, the policeman tried to stamp his heel into his assailant's instep, but the man had anticipated this and stood far enough behind him to make this impossible. How the hell did we get out of this at the Academy? kept running through Molina's brain. He was on the verge of blacking out, and he knew it. Then, while bright lights flashed in his eyes and head, he remembered. He loosed his grasp on the attacker's wrists, where he had been struggling in vain to break the grip, and brought his hands back to his own neck. Finding the hands that were throttling him—My God, if they were any closer together, they could clap, he thought—his numb fingers found what they were looking for. The little fingers. The pinkies, Molina remembered calling them when he was a child. Wrenching, twisting them backward, he felt one of them snap out of its socket. The other was precariously at the point of fracturing.

"Yaaargh," Carrington screamed and released the pressure he had held on Molina's throat. The policeman quickly turned, still on the brink of fainting, and with all his remaining strength, lunged his right hand into Carrington's solar plexus. The man doubled up and fell to the ground.

The other officer was coming forward at a dead run. He was there within ninety seconds.

"Call Lieutenant Zimmerman," Molina croaked as he stood over the fallen man, the words barely audible from his raw throat. "Tell him we've got something to hold Carrington on. Attempted murder."

Chapter Forty-five The police, however well-intentioned and duty-bound, could be a bunch of clods, Brian Collier was thinking as he interviewed Frederick Coldter in the youth's cell. Here was a man just managing to keep his emotional balance in what would have been even for a healthy person an extremely difficult situation. The police had been warned by the fellow's doctor that the patient was not well. Yet they persisted in hounding him. If Coldter did go over the edge, the police would have only themselves to blame.

But again, blame is an act of retribution. There is nothing constructive about it. If Sergeant Donofrio, for example, were busted a grade for his manhandling of Coldter, it would not bring the youth back to sanity.

But the psychiatrist's immediate problem was to keep these speculations on an academic level. Frederick Coldter had begun to manifest further signs of slipping away from reality, and Collier was using all his skills to keep the young man in this world that we seem to find preferable. Certainly, Collier was forced to agree to himself, the insulated, comfortable existence into which Coldter was being tugged, the world in which his wife had never been brutally murdered and he had never been put in jail, was more attractive at the moment. Of course, an additional problem faced the doctor. He himself could not say for certain what was real and what was fantasy in Coldter's story. When he insisted that he knew nothing of the murder of his bride of four months, and convinced the doctor that he believed this, was this a fact, or had he merely blotted the brutal memory from his mind? When he insisted that a mysterious man had helped him back to the apartment, after he found the body, was this a figment of his imagination? The facts seemed to indicate that it was.

A bitter memory coursed through the doctor's mind. It had not happened to him, but to a colleague—a man he knew, liked, and respected. It had happened a few years back up in Spanish Harlem. A man, a Puerto Rican in his early thirties, had been brought in for grievous assault on his wife. He claimed that his wife had a lover, who had thrown him out of his bed and forced him to sleep in the kitchen. This would have been believable enough. But the man insisted that the lover drank blood, and forced his wife to do the same. He was brought in in a state of extreme excitement, and his story had been written off as the ravings of a sick mind. It was not until three years later—three years in which the man had been incarcerated in an institution—that he convinced a lawyer at least to investigate the case. Sure enough, when the lawyer visited the apartment, he found that the lover, now the substitute husband, was in the habit of cutting his arm and dripping his own blood into his beer. It gave him virility, he claimed. The man who had been wrongly institutionalized was released, but it was a while before he could come to grips with the outside world again.

Now Dr. Collier was attempting to strengthen his own patient's tenuous hold on reality. This was particularly difficult because Coldter did not seem too keen on hanging on. The Coldters' marriage, it seemed, had not been all that the romantic novels had promised. They both drank too much, they had fought—severely on occasion —and they had not even managed to find an escape from this antagonism in bed. As they talked, Collier got a clearer and clearer picture of what was going on in Coldter's mind. The young man was not actively fighting the charges against him, because he believed himself at least partially responsible for what had happened. On occasion he had indeed wished that his wife were dead, or at least that he would be rid of her. Now that she was out of the picture, he could not escape the feeling that this had happened in response to his morbid wishes.

In the middle of one of these revelatory reveries, a commotion arose in the hallway outside the cell. Both doctor and patient rose and looked out through the bars to see what was happening. Two policemen and a guard were escorting a manacled prisoner to a cell. The man was screaming, "Get me a doctor. My hands are broken. The bastard broke my hands."

"You'll get a doctor as soon as you quiet down," the guard informed him. "There aren't enough doctors in this city for you to try to kill one of them, too."

Collier turned from the scene, and sat down at the foot of the cot. But Coldter remained at the bars, staring at the quartet until they were out of his line of sight. Still, he stood thoughtfully at the cell door.

"Doctor," he began as he slowly turned, "I'm not positive, but I could almost swear that that was the man who helped me that night. I really think that was the same man."

Chapter Forty-six   Donofrio and Lieutenant Zimmerman were in the latter's office when, less than twenty minutes later, Brian Collier revealed this latest development. Zimmerman merely smiled.

"That's another cup of coffee you owe me, Bob," he

said. "I had a feeling that holding on to Coldter would be a good idea."

"A good idea?" the doctor stormed. "Let me tell you something, Al. Every hour we keep him in that cell, every minute we let him think of himself as a criminal, that young fellow moves further and further away from sanity. He blames himself for his wife's death, and you are agreeing with him. That's all he needs."

"What do you mean, agreeing with him?" Zimmerman demanded. "He's been charged with suspicion of murder. Not murder. We never accused him of doing anything, except lying to us."

"That's not the point, and you know it," the psychiatrist rebutted. "He used to fight with his wife. That's how he got that scar. Okay. A perfectly understandable reason to lie, when you find out that she's been stabbed and strangled to death, don't you think? The point is, though, that because they used to fight, and because he used to fantasize her dead, he's beginning to think that he did kill her. A little while longer, and he'll have convinced himself. That's the risk you're running with your 'good ideas.' Now you let him out of there."

Zimmerman sat silently for a long moment, staring at his hands outstretched on the desk in front of him.

"Okay, Doc," he finally conceded. "You do one thing for us, and we'll cooperate with you. One more thing we want from Coldter, and then he's free to go home."

"What's that?"

Zimmerman shuffled through his desk drawers and pulled out a dozen four-by-five-inch photographs—all passport-type pictures, a few with prison numbers stenciled across the subjects' chests. Among them, one of seven pictures of men in business suits without numbers, was a year-old photograph of Roger Carrington. They had found the original in the apartment, and had since used this portrait for distribution to the Homicide Squads in all five boroughs, and to the men actually involved in the investigation.

He shuffled the pictures, mixing them up like playing cards, then handed them to the doctor. "Here's what we're going to do. You and I are going to pay a visit on Mr. Coldter. You are going to show him these pictures. If he picks out Carrington as the man who helped him back to his apartment on the night of the murder, we'll let him go. Fair enough?"

"Fair enough," the doctor responded.

"But one thing, Brian. We want you to have a talk with him after I leave. Keep him as a voluntary patient, if you have to. I want him to be able to testify at Carrington's trial. Agreed?"

"Agreed."

Frederick Coldter was hailing a cab for home less than an hour later.

Chapter Forty-seven "Well, Brian," Zimmerman began after the doctor had re-entered his office, following the release of Frederick Coldter. "Now all you have to worry about is Carrington."

"How do you mean?" the doctor asked.

"Well, I'm convinced that he's the murderer. We've managed to trace a really elaborate plan he followed to get in and out of the country in time to commit each of the murders. His own description of their relationship when he came in here the first time, voluntarily, establishes the fact that he had ample motive to kill his wife.

On top of that, we checked with his bank and with his family lawyer, the one who handles the estate he derives that income of his from, and he couldn't have possibly afforded to pay the alimony that the court established and still keep up his standard of living. I mean, my God, the guy got eight hundred dollars a month before taxes, and the alimony was set at five hundred. It's ridiculous. In addition, thanks to Frederick Coldter, we can establish that he was at the scene of one of the crimes at the time it happened. Also, that he had no real reason for being there.

"And as if that isn't enough, he did try to kill Molina. Same way, too. Strangulation. We can hold him as long as we want just on the attempted murder charge.

"In other words, we can already send him away for a long time for attempted murder; we've got a good case there. We've even got a witness—another officer—to testify that he jumped Molina. But we'd like to be able to close the books on the four murders. We've got a good case, but it's all circumstantial. I don't really think we have enough for a conviction.

"What we want you to do, is see if we can get that evidence. I'll tell you the truth; the knowledge that we don't have to worry about these killings is more important to us than a Murder One conviction. At this point, I'd settle to send him to Matteawan. If you say that the State Hospital for the Criminally Insane is where he belongs, I'll go along with it. I'll even try to get the district attorney to do likewise. I'll play ball with you this way, but only under one condition—that you can get enough information out of him to enable us to know with some certainty that he is the mass murderer. Next time I go before the captain, I don't want to have to tell him that I *think* we've got the guy. I want to be able to tell him that I *know* we do."

"That sounds pretty reasonable, Al," the psychiatrist

said. "Particularly considering who's making the offer. I've never known you to be this nice about a case before. You don't have any ulterior motive, do you?"

"Sure I do," Zimmerman said. "If we go through the usual procedure—the trial and the sanity hearings and one group of psychiatrists saying he's crazy and another group saying that he isn't—he could, conceivably, get off scot free. Look at it this way—we're defeating ourselves. If we go after Murder One, we don't have the strongest of cases. And if we did, we'd be arguing that he's sane enough to stand trial. If we won that point, and went on to lose the trial, we'd really be up the creek. After something like that, we might not even be able to make an attempted-murder charge stick. Oh, I can really see it now. Some smartass defense lawyer telling how we hounded poor Carrington until he finally turned on the cop who was following him and attacked him. I don't even know if the D.A. would want to take a case like that to court, if he lost the Murder One trial. God, the newspapers would have a picnic!

"Now, if that happened, Carrington could be back out on the street within a year. And probably suing us for false arrest, to boot.

"If, however, we can get him to implicate himself further in the murders, we can lock him up in a padded cell somewhere and stop worrying about him. The important thing, remember, is that society is protected from the likes of him. I want to accomplish this in the quickest, least risky way possible."

"And what happens," Dr. Collier inquired, "if in a few years, the authorities at Matteawan decide he's fit to go free? People do get cured in mental hospitals, you know. Even the criminally insane."

"I thought of that, too. Then, we can try him for attempted murder. If he's insane now, he can't stand trial anyway. On any charge. We won't, I know, be able to use the evidence that he gives us on the murder charges. A confession like that, if he should decide to give us one, wouldn't stand up in a later trial. Particularly if he's certifiably insane when he makes the confession.

"With the attempted murder rap, though, we've got real evidence. We could get a conviction, even five years from now. Oh, I know he'd probably just draw a suspended sentence. But at least we'd have him on probation where we could keep an eye on him until we're satisfied that he's not going to go around killing people. The district attorney may think he's God's avenging angel, but I've never been able to see myself that way. All I want to do is protect society and close these four murder cases."

"Do you really think you can sell this approach to the district attorney? He's not going to like it one bit, you know."

"He isn't going to have any choice if you can get him certified before he gets his hands on the case."

"True," Dr Collier admitted. "Well, I can't promise you anything, but I'll do what I can with him. Your proposition sounds reasonable enough to me. I'll talk to him. Do you think he should have his lawyer present?"

"Only if he asks for him," Zimmerman said. "And if he does, I want to talk to him first and see if I can sell him on this approach, too. If he's any kind of lawyer, I think he'll go along with it. After all, even attempted murder can get Carrington ten to twenty years."

"Well, Al, I'll see what I can do. I can't promise any more than that. By the way," Dr. Collier said as he was leaving the lieutenant's office, "is there any chance at all that Carrington did *not* commit the murders? I wouldn't

188

want to make a fool out of myself, you know."

"In my mind," Zimmerman answered with authority, "no chance at all. We might not be able to sell it to a jury, but I have absolutely no doubt that he's our man."

"That's good enough for me, Al. I'll do what I can."

Chapter Forty-eight   Any experienced policeman will tell you that he would rather deal with the most violent brutal thug than with a woman who is drunk, irate, or both. Barbara Holdakker was both.

As soon as the word was received that Carrington had been taken into custody, Communications Division, at the behest of Lieutenant Zimmerman, had ordered a squad car to the house in Brooklyn to pick her up for questioning. It sounded like a simple enough request, and the two officers who approached the front door had anticipated little difficulty. They had no way of knowing, however, that the young lady had gone through the better part of a fifth of vodka during the night, and had not, in fact, even gone to bed.

It was this bottle that came flying at their heads when they opened the door, there having been no answer to the repeated knocks. Fortunately for the uniformed officers who had entered the house, the men outside, still on stake-out duty, heard the bottle crash against the wall and rushed in to assist. It had taken all four of them to subdue her.

If a man had behaved that way, the driver thought as they headed back to the station house in Manhattan, Barbara Holdakker manacled in the back seat, they would simply have given him enough of a tap with a night stick to calm him down. Somehow, they couldn't bring themselves to do that with a woman. No policeman could. It was, in a way, irrational on their part—no man they had ever encountered had fought so viciously. Blood had been drawn on the faces of both stake-out detectives, thanks to her nails, and Hodges, the driver's partner, would not be making love to his wife tonight, if that kick had had the effect that he thought it did. He glanced over, and saw that Hodges was still surreptitiously rubbing his stomach just above the groin. The driver himself had escaped relatively without injury. It was not until an hour later that he noticed the matted hair and blood where her hair-pulling had torn his scalp.

Seven hours later, after the young lady had been placed in a solitary cell to overcome the effects of the alcohol, she was in some state approaching normality—or at least rationality. It was at this point that Zimmerman called the women's lockup downstairs and asked that Miss Holdakker be shown up to his office.

"Hello, Miss Holdakker," Lieutenant Zimmerman began. "I hope you're feeling better."

"Blechhh!" she exclaimed. "Have you got a glass of water?"

Donofrio rose and went outside to the water cooler in the squadroom. He returned less than a minute later carrying a small paper cup. Water dripped from his hand, where it had sloshed.

"And a couple of aspirin?" she asked.

Zimmerman dutifully opened his desk and withdrew a pair of tablets from his private stock. Wordlessly, he handed them across the desk to the girl. She popped both into her mouth at once, and quickly drowned them in water. She then held the cup out to Donofrio to be refilled. He did so without having to be asked. When he returned, she grabbed the cup from him and quickly gulped its contents.

"That's a little better," she finally commented. "Although I'll never understand why they make those damn cups so small. God, I think I must have been drinking rubbing alcohol!"

Zimmerman smiled sympathetically. "Hopefully, this won't take too long," he said. "Then you can go back downstairs for a little rest."

"Back downstairs? Back to jail? What have I done? Look, I know I got a little nasty when those cops came barging into the house; but I didn't do anything. Am I under arrest?"

"That's up to you, Miss Holdakker," Zimmerman said firmly.

"How do you mean, it's up to me?"

"As far as the record is concerned, you have not yet been charged with anything. We have several choices. These range all the way from nothing at all—just letting you leave—to accessory after the fact of murder."

"After the fact of *what?*"

"Murder, Miss Holdakker. This is the Homicide Division."

"Who was murdered? I don't know anything about it. I don't know what you're talking about. I never killed anybody."

"We're not accusing you of anything. Not yet, anyway. As things stand now, you may be able to be of some help to us. If you cooperate, there won't be any charges against you. If you don't . . ." He let the sentence hang ominously.

"Hold on for a minute. Please," she implored in an attempt to be rational. "First tell me what this is all about; then, if I do know anything, I'll be glad to tell you."

191

"All right, Miss Holdakker. It's about Roger Carrington. We have very good reason to believe that he is responsible for four murders in this city within the past six weeks. We have some evidence to connect him with a couple of them—those of his wife and of a young girl who was killed two night later. We're trying to connect him with the others. The same method was used to kill the girls, so we have every reason to suspect that Mr. Carrington is responsible for them. But suspicions aren't enough. We want to close the books on those cases, and we need proof."

"The past six weeks? But Roger and I were in Mexico for most of that time. He couldn't have killed anyone in New York. We were in Mexico!"

"No you weren't, Miss Holdakker. We've already broken that alibi. Or should I call you Mrs. Culligan?"

For a long moment, she stared at Zimmerman. Then she said, "Look, questioning me isn't going to help you. I can't tell you anything. Believe me, I didn't have anything to do with whatever Roger was up to when he went away. I didn't know what he was doing, and I didn't want to know. If he hurt anybody, or if, as you say, he killed anybody, I'm sorry. But I didn't have anything to do with it."

"We'd like to believe that, Miss Holdakker."

"Besides, even if I did, I wouldn't be able to help." She paused, as if for effect. "A wife can't testify against her husband, you know."

"A wife? Are you and Carrington married?"

"Yes," she admitted reluctantly. "Three weeks ago in Mexico. I can prove it if I have to. The marriage certificate is back at the house in Brooklyn."

This time it was Zimmerman who paused to think. "You know," he began at last, "what you said isn't entirely true. It's a popular misconception, but it isn't true that a wife can't testify against her husband. The law is that a wife cannot be forced to testify against her husband. She can do so voluntarily, you know."

"Really?" she asked, surprised.

"Yes, that's the law. Would you like to get a lawyer and ask him? He'll tell you the same thing."

"Oh, I see. No, I don't think I'll need a lawyer. What is it you want to know? Believe me, I don't know anything about the murders, if Roger did commit them."

"Well, why don't you start by telling us why you took such a circuitous route from the apartment in St. Paul's Square to the house in Brooklyn last night. That looks pretty suspicious, you know."

"Oh. Well, that was Roger's idea. We were pretty short of money, you see. And Roger said that his ex-wife used to keep fifty or sixty dollars hidden in the apartment. Up on a closet shelf, all the way in the back. So he told me to go there, find it, and bring it home. He said he couldn't go himself because he hated her so much that he didn't even want to set foot in the place. I searched high and low and couldn't find a dime. I must have looked for over an hour.

"I guess it was pretty stupid of me to believe a story like that. Well, to make a long story short, he did say that some private detectives were watching the place to collect some bills. His wife had hired them to watch him while they were still married, and she didn't have the money to pay them. He didn't have the money either, but he said that they were threatening to get tough with him if he showed up. He said she owed them more than a thousand dollars, and he just didn't have it. So he said that if anybody followed me away from the house, I should do my best to lose them. He told me about going uptown, then back downtown and all that. I guess I didn't do a very good job, did I?"

"Good enough," Zimmerman said.

"Well, there wasn't any money hidden in the closet, and he got mad and hit me when I got home. He stormed off to bed, and I took the bottle and decided to drown my sorrows. That's all there is, I guess. I really don't know anything about the murders,"—she paused ruefully—"although frankly I wouldn't put it past him."

"Miss Holdakker—Mrs. Carrington . . ."

"I think I'd prefer Miss Holdakker, if you don't mind."

"Okay, Miss Holdakker, did Mr. Carrington ever tell you what he did when he went out alone at night?"

"No, and I didn't ask. Believe it or not, I trusted him."

"Did he wear the same clothes he usually wore? Did he do anything peculiar? Anything at all that you can think of might be of help to us."

"No, no, he . . . Wait a minute. Yes. Before he went out at night, he would always go down into the basement for a while. Then, he wouldn't come back upstairs to say he was leaving or anything. He'd leave from there. I wouldn't know he was gone until I called him."

"How long did you know Roger Carrington, by the way?"

"Two years," she said in a small, tired voice.

"Two years? Then you knew him before the divorce?"

"Yes, I guess you might as well hear it from me. Somebody else will only tell you sooner or later, any way. Roger didn't spend very much time in St. Paul's Square, you know. He had rented the house in Brooklyn for me. I've only been in Los Angeles once in my life, and that was just for a visit. When I left Des Moines, that's where I went all right, but it didn't take me too long to realize that I wasn't the movie actress I thought I was. I was there for less than a month. I ran out of money, so I took a part in one of those terrible movies—those nudies—

God, I worried for a year that some guy back home might get to see it and recognize me, and tell my folks. Well, that paid me enough to fly to New York and check in at the Y. I took whatever jobs I could get—telephone operator, sales girl—I was even a clerk in the Automat for a few weeks. But no matter where I went, the guys, my bosses, couldn't keep their hands off me. You know, I've got a good figure. I always prided myself on it. When I was fourteen, I was the most popular girl in school. But believe me, it's a curse.

"Well, at any rate, I had one job after another for about a year. A little less, maybe. I moved into a one-room walkup in the Village because it was cheap. Then one day I saw an ad for an artists' model in one of those Village newspapers. I was pretty hard up, and I had already done that movie, so I figured, What the hell? At least there wasn't much of a chance of anybody back in Iowa ever seeing a painting. That's how I met Roger. He was the artist who had advertised. He wasn't too bad, either. I really took a liking to him after a couple of weeks. You know, even while I was posing nude, he never made a pass at me. That was different, all right. For a while I thought he didn't like girls. You know what I mean?"

Zimmerman nodded.

"So, he started taking me to dinner, and I slept in the studio—he had a loft up on Little West Twelfth Street, near the river. Soon he told me to give up my apartment, that he'd found this house in Brooklyn. Nice, respectable neighborhood, and all that. He said he was going to give up the studio, and I could stay in this house and take care of it. That would have been about eighteen months ago. I know this is hard for you to believe, but he didn't even try to make a pass at me until we had been there over a month. By then, I didn't put up any fight, let me tell you.

195

He was the only decent thing that had happened to me since I left Des Moines. Ever since then, that's the way it was. He would come to the house a couple or three days a week, and paint. Sometimes I'd model; other times, he'd do still lifes. Then, it got to be four or five times a week. All the neighbors thought we were married, I suppose.

"When he'd leave at night, I just assumed that he was going back to his apartment. We weren't married then, after all. He still had a wife, even though it was pretty obvious that he couldn't stand her.

"Well, to bring you up to date, a few months ago, he told me that he was divorcing her and he wanted to marry me. Believe me, I didn't argue. I might have been comfortable enough with things like they were, but no girl likes to think she's going to spend her life as a mistress.

"So he went off to Las Vegas—no, it was Reno—and told me he'd take me to Acapulco after the divorce. We were going to get married there, and have a real honeymoon. It sounded all right to me, so that's just what we did.

"Well, you wouldn't believe how much a man could change. He always used to be polite, and nice, and a real gentleman. I tell you, he no sooner slipped that ring on my finger when he turned into a real rat. I never saw him drunk before we were married, and I don't think I saw him sober for two days at a stretch after. That's when he started punching me around. When he was drunk. Last night, when I came in the house without the money, he was sober, but he started hitting me anyway. That's when I decided that maybe I ought to start doing some drinking myself. It's not what it's cracked up to be, believe me."

"What about these times he'd go down to the basement and then leave?" the lieutenant interjected.

"That was fairly recent. He came back from Reno before we went down to Mexico, and that's when it started. He'd never done anything like that before. He used to be such a nice guy. It was just amazing how he changed."

"I can imagine," Zimmerman said, not without sarcasm. "But when you came back from Mexico, why did you use a phony name?"

"Ha." She laughed self-pityingly. "Here's a beaut for you. He told me that he was smuggling in a diamond ring —a surprise for me when we got back to New York. He said that he had already sent stuff to New York that took up the quota you're allowed to bring in duty-free. So he said we'd have to use another name. They never ask for any identification when you come in from Mexico, just as long as you don't speak with an accent. I believed him! Can you beat that? I really believed him!

"Sure," she continued sarcastically, "I'm still waiting for all that stuff he 'sent up from Mexico' to arrive. I'm still waiting for the diamond, too."

She held out her left hand and displayed a large ring on the fourth finger. "I went to a jeweler to have this setting changed. He told me the 'stone' was glass. I never did tell Roger, because I thought he was cheated and I didn't want to hurt his feelings. Boy, what a chump I am. How can one girl be so stupid?"

"Miss Holdakker, all this has been very interesting. But it hasn't helped us too much. Isn't there anything you can tell us that would implicate Mr. Carrington with these crimes?"

"I told you I really don't know anything about them." She paused for thought. "I don't know. Take a look in the basement of the house in Brooklyn. Maybe he hid his little hatchet there."

"We'll do that, Miss Holdakker." Zimmerman said politely. "Now why don't you go back downstairs and take a rest? I'm sure we'll be able to let you go by the time you wake up." He pressed the buzzer on his desk. The door opened and Detective Clancy stuck his head in. "Yes, Lieutenant?"

"Pat, I'd like you to escort Miss Holdakker back to the women's cells. Get her a good one. Private and quiet. She needs a rest."

Chapter Forty-nine   It took slightly more than three hours of searching for the police to find what they were looking for. Behind a stack of packing crates, dusty and spider-webbed from lack of disturbance, they found a suitcase that showed no signs of its surroundings. A cheap, imitation-leather one-suiter, available in any discount store, and frequently advertised as a loss-leader, it was so much newer and cleaner than the boxes and packages around it that the detective who was looking in that section of the Brooklyn basement went right to it as soon as he entered the area of the search. Opening it, he recoiled in disgust. A sweet smell of mildewy clothes and dried blood rose from the suitcase like a genie from a bottle.

Two hours later, the crime laboratory, which had dropped its more routine work to do an immediate analysis, reported that the clothes—a pair of woolen trousers, a dress shirt, and a light coat—bore traces of three types of human blood: O positive, matching that of Mrs. Carrington and Mrs. Coldter; A positive, matching Jane Coleman, and A negative, corresponding to that of Miss Corbin. Carrington's own blood type, they had previously determined, was AB positive. This was evidence.

By four o'clock that afternoon, when Dr. Collier returned to Lieutenant Zimmerman's office to inform him that he would cooperate and arrange to have the suspect committed to a mental institution, the lieutenant was in possession of this latest finding.

"Oh, hello, Brian," Zimmerman said when the psychiatrist entered. "I'm afraid I've got some bad news for you."

"Oh?" Collier asked suspiciously.

"Yeah. I don't think I'll be able to honor my offer to let you institutionalize Carrington."

"Jesus Christ!" the doctor exclaimed. "I work with the guy all day to get him to go along with it, and now you tell me that it's no soap. Why the hell not? You can't use anything he told me anyway. I am a doctor, not a cop. I didn't even ask if he wanted his lawyer present."

"We've got new evidence. We can connect Carrington with the crimes well enough to bring him to trial on Murder One. I don't think the district attorney will settle for any less now."

"That's beautiful. That's just dandy, isn't it?" the doctor declared disgustedly. "Well let me tell you something. The reason I came up here. Carrington just confessed."

"Why that's wonderful!"

"Not for you it isn't. That confession was exacted as part of a deal. I told him that if we could close the books on these murders, that he would be placed in an institution. I told him that he would not have to stand trial for his crimes."

"But Doc, you had no right to do that. That's the D.A.'s decision. Nobody else's."

"Don't tell me I had no right to do it. You gave me your word. You set the terms of this deal, I didn't!"

"Yeah," Zimmerman admitted. "I guess I did." He paused and stared at the pencils stacked on his desk. He picked one up and tested its point with his finger. "Now what the hell are we going to do?"

"I'll tell you what you're going to do. You're going to keep your word," Dr. Collier demanded, "district attorney or no.

"Look, Al," the doctor said, his voice softening, "you really don't have any choice in the matter. Aside from the fact that you gave your word, and all that, I'd have had to recommend Carrington's commitment anyway. That man is, to use your kind of expression, as mad as a hatter. If the district attorney brought this case to trial, even if he had nine positive eye-witnesses for each murder, he'd never get a conviction. The defense would plead insanity, and they wouldn't have any trouble proving it. My God, I'd have to testify to that myself, if they asked me to."

"Really? You really think he's crazy?" Zimmerman asked hopefully.

"No question about it. None whatever. Roger Carrington is schizophrenic. It's written all over him. A first-year medical student could diagnose it, and he'd be right. The guy is a textbook case."

"Let me ask you something, Doc," Sergeant Donofrio interjected. He had been sitting quietly in the rear of the office observing and noting the proceedings. "If he's nuts, how come he set up such an elaborate plan? It was obviously a well-thought-out series of crimes."

"Being 'nuts,' as you so quaintly put it, does not prevent a man from being logical. Adolf Hitler was one of the classic paranoids of our day, and he was logical enough to damn near conquer the world."

"What about the M'Naghten rule?" the sergeant asked. "Didn't he know that he was doing wrong when he committed the murders?"

Dr. Collier smiled, as if he were about to impart a great

truth that he had discovered. "No, he didn't. It's interesting, actually. Peter Volker was, in a way, right. The initials. The J.C.s? Well, they *were* deliberate. Oh, Volker was wrong about the religious aspects of those initials, all right. Religion had nothing really to do with it. But the fact that all the girls had the same initials was Carrington's way of telling us that he was the killer. He wanted to be caught just as much as that guy in Chicago who used to leave those 'Catch me before I kill again' notes on his victims."

"I don't get it," Zimmerman said. "How was that supposed to tell us that Carrington was the murderer?"

The psychiatrist grinned broadly. As a nonpoliceman attached to the Department, few things gave him greater pleasure than beating his comrades at their own game.

"Don't you see," he offered, "Mrs. Carrington's initials were J.C., right?"

"So?"

"What were the initials of her maiden name?

"Don't bother," Collier said as Zimmerman reached for the Carrington file. "They were J.C., also. Janet Cadanovici."

Zimmerman shrugged. "Does that prove Carrington committed the crimes?"

Indulgently, the doctor explained, "Have you ever known a girl who married someone with the same last initial as hers? People notice it. There are all sorts of remarks about her not having to change the monograms on her towels and handkerchiefs, and things like that. The guy's friends will kid him about being too cheap to change a laundry mark. That type of thing. The girl's mother gives them the family silver and remarks that the initial doesn't have to be changed. Believe me, as petty as it may seem, if two people with the same last initial get married, they're both aware of the fact that they have the same last initial. I know it sounds trivial, but this was one small part of Carrington's relationship with his wife, and he was conscious of it. He seized on the initials as a way of tipping you off that it was he who was committing the murders. Remember, as I said before, the vast majority of criminals want to be caught. But only an insane man would try to actually lead you to himself like this."

Zimmerman nodded, indicating that this was, in fact, an approach that he had overlooked. "Now," he began resignedly, "why don't you explain why Carrington committed the murders in the first place?"

"Don't put yourself down, Al. You knew about this initial business all along. When you think about it, it really was the initials thing that led you to Carrington, wasn't it? You checked the initials on the airlines' passenger lists, the initials at the hotels, at the addresses you investigated . . . You knew that they had some significance, even if you weren't quite sure just what that significance was. In a way, you picked up the clue that Carrington offered you and did exactly what he wanted."

Zimmerman grinned. "I sure wish I had known it at the time. It would have made things a lot simpler."

The policeman paused, then spoke. "But about Carrington's motive . . . ?"

"Okay," the doctor said. "Start with the premise that Carrington and his wife hardly had what you might call a loving relationship, particularly in the bedroom. He told you as much when he came in to see you that time. Well, to make a long story short, he was in the market for some action—some physical fulfillment. So he struck up his relationship with Barbara Holdakker.

"He told us about that, too. He didn't touch her for quite a while after he knew her, because he liked her. It sounds paradoxical, but it really isn't. Remember, sex was a very painful, tainted experience with his wife. When he did start sleeping with the Holdakker girl, he was made to suffer all sorts of guilt feelings. His wife's attitude had seen to that. Finally, he saw through the smoke screen that his wife had created, and he realized that a good, well-balanced sexual relationship was not in itself necessarily painful. It was only his wife who had made it seem that way.

"Well, that was the turning point. He was on the fence —he could have, at that point, cured himself if he could have accepted his new relationship without thinking back on the old. Instead, however, he tumbled. He developed a real, active hatred for his wife for what she had turned their own relationship into. By withholding herself from him as she had done, she altered his view of all women. At least, all the women with whom he associated sex.

"Thus, although his wife was the prime target—you were right there, Al—*all* women were evil. He picked the Corbin girl, his first killing, for two reasons. First, she was in the habit of smiling at him on the way to the subway in the morning. They apparently left at about the same time, when he went anywhere that is, and they knew each other's faces. He decided that she was flirting, that she was trying to seduce him. Her initials—they had introduced themselves in the park one Sunday—made it worse. He followed her that night from her office. She had a date. She went up to the guy's apartment, and it infuriated him that she might be making love. When she came down, a little while later, he was determined to kill her. He took a cab back home, and waited for her in the alley. You know the rest.

"The second reason he killed her was as a wife-substitute. He was, as it were, practicing. Besides, he did want

203

to establish this pattern of insane killings so that he could try to get away with it. He knew that if he had just murdered his wife, the police would go directly to him. So he tried to establish a chain, and send you off looking for someone without any real motive.

"Jane Coleman, the next girl he killed, was something else entirely. He claims that he never met her before, but I rather suspect that he might have seen her in her professional capacity. He might have been a client, as it were. That would explain the initials coincidence.

"But even if he didn't know her, she still fits the pattern. A woman who is easily associated with his view of sex and women. In fact, a prostitute. A likely choice for the second link in his chain. He had read a little about Jack the Ripper, who liked to prey on women of the street, and he knew that we wouldn't be able to connect him with her death. He picked her up, as any man might pick up a girl like her, and led her down to the basement in his old building. There, he killed her, took her body out into the church yard, and mutilated it.

"Now we come to the murder of his wife. He felt he had built a long enough chain of murders to set a precedent. However much of a motive he might have, he felt he could avoid detection while the police were looking for another Boston strangler type. He didn't realize, of course, that he was this type of psychotic himself."

"But, Brian," Lieutenant Zimmerman broke in, "again, wouldn't the fact that he tried to avoid being caught, even if it was in this bloody way, indicate that he did know that he was committing crimes? That would qualify him for trial, as far as the courts are concerned."

"No, Al. That's where his mental aberration took over. While he was trying to cover his tracks and create alibis with one hand, he was begging us to catch him with the other. It's characteristic of these cases."

"Begging us to catch him? What are you talking about? He sure didn't leave many clues."

"Didn't he? Maybe we couldn't see them, but they were there, all right. Look, why do you think he took the Coleman girl, the prostitute, into the basement of his own house? And then he deposited her right across the street. He could easily have hauled her further down the block. The same way, there was absolutely no sign of breaking and entering in his apartment when he killed his wife. He knew that this would tell us that the murderer was somebody she knew. And the biggest factor of all, of course, was when he walked in here and offered to help us. If you had turned to him right then and there and told him you knew he had done it, and if you had been able to throw in a few facts to substantiate that claim, he would have confessed all over the place. That's what he just did with me."

"At the time, we didn't know, though," Zimmerman admitted.

"Oh, I know that. I'm not saying you should have confronted him. I'm only postulating what he would have done if you had."

"Is this business of him wanting to be caught the reason he hung around the Coldter apartment after the crime?" Donofrio asked.

"Exactly," the psychiatrist exclaimed, visibly delighted that the sergeant had caught the train of thought. "Why, he even offered to call the police for Coldter. You notice, though, that he got out of there pretty quickly when Coldter said he'd do it himself. Hell, Carrington's an intelligent man. He surely would have known that Coldter would have been able to identify him. He was daring us to figure out who he was."

"It's all so easy when you know who did it," Zimmerman commented sarcastically.

"Sure, Al. I know this is Monday-morning quarterbacking, but let me finish. The one that threw you, the one that led you to suspect that there was more than one murderer, was the Coldter case. This was where he slipped, frankly. It was out of the pattern, and I think he knew it. That's why he went to ground. When he got on that bus in Brooklyn yesterday, that was the first time he had gone out of the house in over a week. He had violated his own pattern in a couple of ways, and for a couple of reasons. Remember, this crime was committed much more publicly than any of the others. The first was in a dark alley, the second in a basement, his wife was killed in their own apartment. But the Coldter girl was killed in a place where somebody could have stumbled on them at any time. All anybody else on that floor had to do was open his door."

"But why did Carrington have to kill her at all?" Donofrio asked. "After all, his wife, the one who supposedly keyed all this up, the reason for his rampage, was already dead."

"That's exactly why he had to do it," the doctor explained. "If he had stopped after he killed his wife—and he *did* have a good motive, remember—he felt that he would be leading the police right to his door. But he felt if he did just one more job, he'd be throwing us off the track for good. It's true, too. Look at the time that was spent pursuing the Coldter angle.

"Now the Coldter case was different for several reasons. First, as I said, she was killed, more or less, in public. He only stabbed her about half as many times. There are two possible explanations for this. In fact, both may be true. They don't contradict each other. For one thing, he had less time because he could have been easily discovered. Second, and more important, his drive to stab over and over and over, his desire to mutilate, had been lessened now that the real object of his hatred was dead. By the way, that item, the number of stab wounds, should have tipped you off to Carrington a long time ago."

"How do you figure that? If anything, it led us to suspect Coldter," Zimmerman reminded the doctor.

"It shouldn't have. Remember, Janet Carrington was stabbed more and mutilated worse than any of the others. The first two were stabbed almost exactly the same number of times. Coincidence? Perhaps, but not likely. No. He knew what he was doing. And in the process of setting up a pattern, this was an important part. But in the case of his wife, for the first time, he lost control of himself and didn't count the stabs. He just kept going. Now in the Coldter girl's case, he simply cut her up a little; he did not mutilate her as he had the other victims. Nor did he attack her sexual organs, per se.

"Here, too, he varied his pattern on the one hand to throw us off the scent, and on the other, to put us back on it. His desire for self-preservation made him conceal the crimes, but his occasionally stronger need to be punished made him tell us, in however devious a way, how we could find him. As best we can tell, he didn't know her at all; he was simply lurking in the hallway. This is the one case where the initials may have been a coincidence. I don't know. Either way it makes sense.

"A crime of opportunity, you might call it," the psychiatrist went on. "Carrington had to commit one more murder, as I said.

"As nearly as I can figure it out, piecing together what he told me, he sneaked into the apartment house to choose his victim simply because it was the easiest place in the area to enter unobserved. Remember, there are a lot of apartments in that building. A lot of traffic goes through that front door. And as long as you don't look suspicious, the doorman isn't going to stop you.

"So he walked into the building and rode up in the elevator. He told me that he just closed his eyes and pushed a floor button. The first floor he went to was eight, but there was a party going on up there and he was afraid that too many people might be coming and going, so he got out of the elevator, found the stairs, and went down one flight. A credit card slipped into the bolt was all he needed to open the exit door. He saw Mrs. Coldter in the incinerator room as soon as he got the door open. You know the rest."

The psychiatrist paused to survey the effect of his tale on the two policemen.

"There, gentlemen," he finally continued, "is your case. There isn't a psychiatrist in the country, myself included, who would judge Carrington sane enough to stand trial. You don't have any choice but to allow us to commit him."

Chapter Fifty   Once a month, the first assistant district attorney meets with the assembled police captains in his jurisdiction to be briefed on what cases he could expect to come in for prosecution in the foreseeable future. Usually the captains report, precinct by precinct, while he takes notes, only occasionally asking a question. This time, however, the routine was broken.

As soon as Assistant D.A. Byron Bruder entered the chilly, sparsely furnished conference room, he asked if

O'Brien had come in yet. Two or three of the captains shrugged their shoulders in reply.

Gathering his courage with a deep breath, Lieutenant Zimmerman stepped forward and confronted the prosecutor.

"Captain O'Brien isn't going to be here today," he began. "He asked me to take his place. I'm Zimmerman."

"I know who you are," the D.A.'s representative responded testily. "What is Mike, sick?"

"No, he's all right. It's just that I've been handling those murders in St. Paul's Square, and we've resolved the case, and he wanted me to tell you about it myself, I guess." The lieutenant smiled weakly. "He wanted you to chew out the right guy."

Bruder's eyebrows went up quizzically. "Chew you out? I thought you just said that the case had been resolved."

"It has been." The lieutenant paused. "But you're not going to be able to bring it to trial."

A look of indignant disgust crossed the assistant D.A.'s face as he stared at the nervous policeman. Finally, he turned his back and strode to the head of the conference table. Turning and seating himself abruptly, he declared: "I think we all better sit down and listen to this. It sounds like it's going to be a beauty."

The captains, who had been clustered behind the junior officer to listen in, spread out around the table and took their seats. They looked up at Zimmerman expectantly.

"Proceed!" the assistant district attorney finally barked.

Deliberately avoiding the prosecutor's eyes, the lieutenant laid out the whole story from start to finish. Nobody interrupted. Nobody asked any questions. Nobody spoke. A few of the other policemen began fidgeting nervously as the speaker detailed his dealings with the psychiatrist.

When Zimmerman finished, some twenty minutes after he had begun, he looked up and was slightly surprised to notice that nobody was looking at him. The assistant district attorney was staring at his hands in front of him on the polished wood of the table.

Slowly, with an apparently massive effort, the prosecutor raised his bald head and brought his eyes to bear on the waiting lieutenant.

"Let me understand this," he began slowly, pronouncing each word deliberately. "*You* made a deal with the prisoner and the psychiatrist not to prosecute this case?"

Zimmerman knew that the rhetorical question was not to be answered, but served as a prologue to the explosion that would follow. He had seen the first assistant district attorney begin this way several times in court. The thought crossed his mind that now he knew how a defendant felt. His throat tickled from twenty minutes of talking, but he knew that he didn't dare cough.

Still, underlying all his feelings of nervousness and the sure and certain knowledge that the district attorney's office was about to give him a proper dressing-down, the lieutenant honestly believed that he had done the right thing. That knowledge did absolutely nothing to relieve his present anxiety.

"I passed the bar examination in 1953," Bruder began, rising from his seat and slowly turning so that his back was to the still-standing Zimmerman. "I first took the exams in 1952, but I only passed one section then, so I had to come back the next year and take a part over." He did a half turn to face the police captain sitting at his immediate right. "So maybe I'm not as smart as some people. Maybe that's why I ended up in the district attorney's office. Because I wasn't bright enough to go into corporation law, or crooked enough to go into negligence, or talented enough or conceited enough to see myself as another Darrow or Nizer or Belli. No, I joined the district attorney's office instead. That was in 1955. Sixteen years ago. Sixteen years."

Suddenly, he swung around, planted his fists solidly on the conference table and faced the lieutenant, glaring.

"But in all those sixteen years I have never heard of anything like this!"

As much as he had steeled himself for the inevitable onslaught, Zimmerman still winced back from the attack.

"Sixteen years of dealing with the Police Department and I have never heard the like of this before." He paused and looked at each face around the room.

"I really don't believe it, you know. A cop and a shrink acting as judge and jury. I really can't believe it. I'll tell you one thing for damn sure, though . . ." He turned back to Zimmerman. "I don't *want* to believe it."

The prosecutor stood staring at the lieutenant, without speaking, for what seemed to Zimmerman a very long time. Wordlessly, he snatched up the papers he had laid out in front of him on the table, and crammed them back into his briefcase. Wheeling around so sharply that he almost knocked over his chair, he stormed to the door.

"We'll meet again on Monday to review your reports," he told the others. A large flake of plaster fell from the ceiling when he slammed the door behind him.

There was an audible sound of expelled breath in the room as the policemen sighed, almost in unison. The slightly shell-shocked lieutenant slumped forward, leaning on his hands on the table.

Slowly, one or two of the captains rose from their seats and left the table. Then they were all on their feet, gathering their notes prior to leaving. Barry Kaplan, the captain in charge of Manhattan Homicide North, paused as he passed behind the still-stunned Zimmerman and put his hand on his shoulder comfortingly.

"You should have known better, Al."

Zimmerman, who had taken about all he could stand for one day, turned sharply.

"What the hell do you mean, Barry? I did the only thing I could do. Collier would have gone into court himself and testified that Carrington was insane. What would you have done?"

"Oh, probably the same thing you did," the captain admitted. "But I would have had the sense not to do it in an election year with a case that would have assured Bruder the district attorney's nomination. You know he's hot for that job."

Zimmerman smiled. "Okay, Barry. Next time we get a maniac like this, I'll write him a little note and ask him to murder women only north of Fifty-ninth Street. Then he'll be your headache."

That same evening Al Zimmerman was driving Bob Donofrio to his house. It was the Zimmermans' turn to entertain the Donofrios.

"I want to show you something, Bob," Zimmerman said as they drove along. He reached into the jacket pocket over his heart and withdrew a sheet of official-looking paper. "Maybe we do need that computer you're always screaming for."

Donofrio took the paper and unfolded it. It was a standard monthly form listing officers who had qualified for promotion, based on examinations passed and time in grade. The names were arranged not alphabetically, as one might expect, but by grade and qualifying rank on the examinations. Under Detective Second Class, the first name on the list was Rodriguez, Miguel.

Neither man spoke for the rest of the trip to the Zim- merman house.